The Heart of a Savage 2

Jibril Williams

Lock Down Publications and Ca$h
Presents
The Heart of a Savage 2
A Novel by *Jibril Williams*

The Heart of a Savage 2

Lock Down Publications
P.O. Box 870494
Mesquite, Tx 75187

Visit our website @
www.lockdownpublications.com

Lock Down Publications
Like our page on Facebook: Lock Down Publications @
www.facebook.com/lockdownpublications.ldp
Cover design and layout by: **Dynasty Cover Me**
Book interior design by: **Shawn Walker**
Edited by: **Jill Alicea**

Jibril Williams

Stay Connected with Us!

Text **LOCKDOWN** to 22828 to stay up-to-date with new releases, sneak peaks, contests and more…

Thank you.

Submission Guideline.

Submit the first three chapters of your completed manuscript to ldpsubmissions@gmail.com, subject line: Your book's title. The manuscript must be in a .doc file and sent as an attachment. Document should be in Times New Roman, double spaced and in size 12 font. Also, provide your synopsis and full contact information. If sending multiple submissions, they must each be in a separate email.

Have a story but no way to send it electronically? You can still submit to LDP/Ca$h Presents. Send in the first three chapters, written or typed, of your completed manuscript to:

LDP: Submissions Dept
Po Box 870494
Mesquite, Tx 75187

DO NOT send original manuscript. Must be a duplicate.

Provide your synopsis and a cover letter containing your full contact information.

Thanks for considering LDP and Ca$h Presents.

Jibril Williams

CHAPTER 1

Racks felt numb to her core. So many emotions ran through her. She missed her cousin dearly and she swiped her tears away with her knuckles. The sour diesel burned slow in the tightly-rolled Backwoods leaf she grasped between her fingers. The clouds of smoke that danced off the burning cannabis created a phantom that hovered over her head.

Normally Racks was the type to keep her emotions in check, but sitting inside Harmony Cemetery was too overwhelming for her. She hated that she couldn't maintain her composure in front of her OG, Whip. She didn't want him to think her shedding tears was a show of weakness. Racks' tears were out of love for her fallen comrade.

"Aye, you know that shit wasn't your fault, right? I been seeing you take the little homie's death the hardest outta all of us. I don't want you to let the homie's death weigh on your conscience," Whip spoke over the Shy Glizzy lyrics that trickled through the speakers of his Charger.

Ranks didn't utter a reply. She inhaled on the Backwoods deeply, holding the diesel hostage in her lungs. Everyone claimed it wasn't her fault her cousin Gunz got killed in a botched robbery, but Racks thought otherwise. It was her mission they went on, so she felt responsible.

Not being able to hold the smoke captive any longer, Racks let the smoke seep from her nostrils and mouth, filling the car with thick clouds. "I hear ya talking, Whip, but we both know better," Racks finally replied as she watched a group of mourners dispersing from a nearby grave.

Four nicely-shaped women remained standing at the open grave, staring down at the lid of their loved one's casket. It seemed they were saying their final goodbyes. Racks wondered, when it was her time to punch the clock, would the homies linger back at her grave to say their final farewells.

Whip let out a deep breath of frustration. He kinda figured Racks was feeling like this by the way she'd been carrying on lately. "Racks, you can't let this situation consume you. The little homie's blood is not on your hands. That shit's on the nigga Spoon's hands. He's responsible, and he will pay for his negligence with his life."

A few months ago, Racks and two Blood homies went out on a mission to rob a gas station to secure money to help filter into their cause of building an organized Blood family called D.C. Bloods – better known as Death Capital Bloods. This branch was a new set of Bloods looking to build a foundation and gain a stronghold in the nation's capital. The problem with the D.C.B. was that while they got the blessing to start the new set of Bloods from the triple OG's back out west, they didn't get the financial backing, so they had to start from the ground up. The D.C. Bloods was lacking funding for their cause. With this being an issue, Whip and Boot mandated everyone had to bring in some kind of money to finance their movement. Once that was established, Whip could better organize his Blood set.

This is what had motivated Racks, Spoon, and Gunz to rob the gas station. Spoon's job was to check the back of the gas station for any employers and nab the security footage, and Racks and Gunz were to hold the clerk at bay and hit the drop box the clerk dropped the daily cash in, along with the money the customers paid for their lotto tickets.

The trio had a solid plan, but Spoon neglected to check the restroom, where the owner was taking a shit. The owner heard the commotion, grabbed his Mossberg pump, and went to confront the robbers. The Amoco owner caught Racks and the homies leaving out the gas station door and a brutal gun battle erupted, leaving the owner shot and a Metropolitan Officer dead right along with Racks' cousin, Gunz.

Racks took another drag off the Backwoods before she passed it to Whip. Every month since Gunz was murdered, Racks came to visit his grave. She would not let his memory die.

The sky opened up with lightning. The lightning made Racks cringe a little as a light drizzle started to fall. The rain pelted against the car's window, creating a soft popping sound.

Two of the four women looked familiar who stood at the gravesite, Racks thought to herself as she focused more on the women.

Two black GMC's pulled up behind the Charger. Something about the trucks didn't sit right with Whip and Racks. Their street instincts kicked in automatically. Racks thought it was 12 until she saw the four men bail out of the trucks. The way they were moving was screaming goons.

One of the women heard the truck doors slam. As she turned around, Racks caught a glimpse of her face. "Tata!" Racks whispered.

The goons drew their bangers, and the cemetery became a battlefield just that quick.

Boom-boom-boom!

Bloka-bloka!

*****

Phatmama pulled her Glock like an expert at the approaching men. They all did the same without hesitation. Phatmama's Glock barked. It sent a hollow-point barreling into one of the approaching men's chin, stopping him in his tracks with his gun still in his hand. Another gunman discharged his gun rapidly. He sent bullets whizzing past Phatmama's head.

The women took cover. Phatmama hid behind a huge statue of an angel with its hands folded in prayer. Tata hit the ground, knocking dirt and grass into her face. A gunman unloaded his weapon at Jelli. Tata rolled over on her left and fell into the open grave, landing on top of Rico's casket. She winced in pain as her back slammed against the coffin top. She struggled to pull her Glock.

Bloka, bloka, bloka, bloka, bloka!

Boom, boom, boom!

Two goons viciously tried to plug Jelli and Zoey with murderous slugs from their 45s. Jelli and Zoey scrambled hard on the ground for cover. There wasn't too much that could protect them from the wrath of the shell showers except the three or four tombstones that rose out of the ground, marking the resting places of the dead.

Zoey was determined not to be another dead soul in Harmony Cemetery. She fell flat on her stomach and rolled over onto her back, bringing her Glock 19 up in one swift motion and letting the trigger ride. A bullet found its home in the shooter's kneecap, which led him to scream out in agony.

"Agh!" He fell to his knees.

Zoey sat up and rocketed him into a world of darkness with a single shot to the forehead. *Boom*!

Jelli finger-fucked her gun with the 30-round extender. Her bullets couldn't find their marks on her attackers. This was her first shootout, and she was scared shitless, but that same fear kept her pulling the trigger on her gun. *Boom, boom, boom*!

Zoey sent a slug into another goon's chest, knocking him sideways into Rico's grave. The goon crashed hard against the top of Rico's casket, knocking the wind out of him. He struggled, trying to get some oxygen into his blood-filling lungs. The goon's hand trembled as he placed his fingers where Zoey's bullets had hit him. He brought them away with blood coating his fingertips. He still struggled to breathe. He began to choke on his own blood.

A beautiful figure appeared over him. He thought God had sent him a beautiful angel to bring him home. Then he was looking down Tata's pink Glock. Tata tapped her trigger, and a spark jumped from her gun like a camera flash. The bullet smashed into the bridge of the killer's nose, splattering the back of his brains on Rico's casket.

Phatmama fell to the ground. She pushed back on her heels and hands, frantically trying to get away from her soon-to-be killer. The gunmen stood over her with murderous eyes. She knew the look way too well because she, too, was a killer. Her heart banged against her chest hard, just like the Drug Task Force's battering ram bangs against a trap house door.

The killer clenched his Taurus 45 tightly while pointing it at Phatmama. "This is fo' Rocco, bitch."

Hearing Rocco's name made the current situation so vivid. *How the fuck this shit came back to haunt me?* thought Phatmama. She closed her eyes, ready to accept her fate like the certified bitch she was.

Boom, boom!

The loud sound cracked over the cemetery like thunder in the sky. Phatmama braced herself for the impact from the killer's bullets, but they never came. The only thing Phatmama felt was the weight of her killer's body crashing on top of her. Blood from the missing portion of the killer's head dripped down onto her face.

Racks stood locked in her shooting stance with her fo'-fo' still smoking in her hand.

Jelli and Zoey ran over to Phatmama, helping to get the corpse off of her. Jelli quickly checked Phatmama's body for any damages.

"I'm good. Where's Tata? And who the fuck is that?" Phatmama said, nodding toward Whip and Racks, who were walking up.

Zoey saw Racks and ran, jumping into her arms and wrapping her legs around Racks' waist. Zoey was still clutching her gun.

"Tata fell in the grave!" Jelli said, helping Phatmama up. "And if it wasn't for them, your ass woulda been dead. Come on! Let's get Tata and get the fuck out of here!"

They found Tata in a crouching position with her gun pointing up at the opening of the grave. Her eyes grew with relief once she saw her girls still standing, but she was confused to see Racks and her bifocal-wearing friend. Zoey scanned the cemetery for any more trouble while Whip helped Tata out of the grave. She saw a white Lexus slowly cruise by and make an exit out of the cemetery.

Police sirens wailed in the distance. The group sprinted back to their cars, not wanting to be there when the police arrived.

Jibril Williams

CHAPTER 2

"What the fuck happened at the cemetery? Who the fuck was them niggas that was trying to kill us? Anybody got any damn clue?" Tata asked with a glass of Henny in her hand. She desperately needed a drink to calm her nerves. The unexpected shootout had the adrenaline pumping hard in her body. Tata studied the room, searching the faces of her Red Bottom Clique and the two outsiders.

They'd made a beeline back to Phatmama's apartment after the shootout. Phatmama sat on the loveseat. Her mind was in another place and time, her thoughts too preoccupied with how Rocco's people found her to be paying attention to what Tata was talking about. Her thoughts were on what their next move was going to be, where it would come from, and if they knew where she laid her head.

Zoey sat next to Racks with her head buried in the palms of her hands. She was trying to wrap her mind around the fact that she had killed two people in one day. Racks rubbed Zoey's back, trying to bring some type of comfort.

No one answered Tata's inquiries. Silence lingered in the air like the smoke rising from Jelli's Backwoods wrap. Jelli was suspicious of Racks, along with her friend, whom she introduced as Whip. Jelli always had a dislike for Racks from the first day they encountered one another, and she damn sure wasn't going to embrace anybody associated with a stud-looking bitch. She didn't give a fuck if she had saved Phatmama's life or not.

"So, why you and your boy was at the cemetery? I find it bizarre you were there," Jelli questioned.

"First, my name ain't 'Boy'! Boy played on Tarzan. And we don't owe you no fucking explanation about why we was there," Whip checked Jelli. He could hear the suspicion in Jelli's line of questioning.

Before Jelli could reply, Racks spoke up. She didn't want any tension with the group of women she was in the room with. She was in debt to Tata. "We just got through visiting my li'l cousin's grave. That's why we was at the cemetery," Racks stated as she looked at Jelli.

Whip was in his body that the li'l homie was explaining herself to an ungrateful, big-titty bitch.

"So, it just so happens we was at the right place at the right time, just like you and Tata was that day me and my homies was at that gas station and shit turned sour for us." Racks was reminding Jelli it was a favor for a favor, one hand washes the other.

Jelli caught on to the message and nodded her head up and down. Jelli remembered the gas station incident way too well, and if it wasn't for Tata's empowered female movement she was on, she would have left Racks' MA-looking ass to get caught by 12. There was something about the tattoo-faced dyke that Jelli wasn't feeling.

Tata walked over and extended her hand toward Racks and Whip. The softness of Tata's hand ignited something inside Whip. Just that quick, he would love to have tasted her chocolate drop, he thought to himself.

"Thank you both for saving us. I don't know if it was God or just a coincidence, but whatever it was, I'm honored you was there, and most definitely I respect your gunplay and your G!" Tata said, giving Racks a pound.

"I was just returning the favor," Racks retorted.

Whip didn't respond. He just pushed his bifocals back on the bridge of his nose.

"I appreciate it. But apparently, someone wants us dead." Tata waved her hand that held the glass with the Henny in it, making the ice cube in her glass clack against the glass. "As of right now, we don't know who these people are. We don't want to bring you into something when we don't fully understand the measure of the situation, so we won't feel some type of way if you excuse yourselves from our madness."

Whip loved the choice of words used when Tata spoke. In his eyes, she had the mannerisms of a Boss Bitch, plus she was sexy as fuck. Her chocolate skin and juicy lips reminded him of Juju from *Love & Hip Hop*. But he could not allow himself or Racks to get involved in whatever the four beauties had going on. He had a Blood line to birth. "You right, and we'll be going," Whip stated, standing up and adjusting the all-red Nationals hat on his head. "Let's ride, Racks."

14

"Hold up for a minute. Let's —"

"This shit isn't Blood business. Let's roll. I'm not getting D.C.B. into something we didn't start or know nothing about. I have twenty Bloods under my umbrella, and I'm not getting them tied up in some shit that don't have shit to do with us. Now you paid your debt to these people, so let's bounce. I spoke on it, and this shit is not open for discussion," Whip spoke aggressively to Racks, showing the room his dominance over her.

Racks lifted herself from the leather sofa where Zoey sat next to her. Zoey gave Whip the Evil Eye.

Jelli held a smile on her face. She loved how Whip handled Racks, and to see Racks come into compliance was priceless to Jelli. She wanted to burst out in laughter.

Tata was feeling a certain way for how Whip barked on Racks, but held her tongue.

Racks walked over to Tata and grabbed her phone from the table. After she punched in a few numbers, she handed the phone to Tata. "I programmed my number in your phone. Stay in touch," Racks said, giving Tata eye contact that said, *Call me. I'm there for you if you need me.*

Racks left with Whip on her heels. The departure of Racks and Whip left an awkward presence in the room, but Phatmama was too consumed with her thoughts to notice. However, the other women felt it.

Tata poured herself another drink and intercepted the Backwoods from Jelli. "I think that whoever them niggas at the cemetery were, they was following us," Tata spoke and broke the silence in the room. She took a long pull of the Backwoods.

This allegation made the Red Bottom Clique search their memory banks for anything that looked questionable when they departed the funeral home off Good Hope Road and headed to Harmony Cemetery. All the women came up blank.

"Could there be someone who knew about us killing Rico? Or do you think Rico called someone and let them know we was meeting with him the night we killed him?" Zoey asked.

"I don't think so, *mami*," Tata said as the smoke leaked from her mouth as she spoke. "Rico was too paranoid to have called someone other than me. Rico thought the Feds was on his ass about the Fed murder that took place at the McCormick Heist. The only person who knew about the heist and us meeting Rico was Rauf. But I don't see why Rauf would want to avenge Rico's death. Rico's and Rauf's relationship was based strictly on business." Tata hit the Backwoods again and chased it with a sip of Henny.

"What about Diesel?" Jelli chimed in.

"I don't know. I haven't seen or heard from Diesel. I haven't heard from him since the Feds raided me and Rico's house, but I'm going to pay this nigga a visit to check his temperature. I know he knows Rico is dead, and he'll be trying to reach out to me soon and figure out where Rico had his stash from the jewelry heist hidden so he can get his cut."

"It's so hard to figure who wants us dead when we can't even see who our enemy is," Jelli said, shaking her head in frustration.

"Trust, what is in the dark will come to the light, *mami*," Tata said.

Hearing that last statement brought Phatmama out of her trance and had her thinking she should tell her companions what she knew about the shootings, but with Jelli being in the room with them, it made her apprehensive. She loved Jelli like a sister, but Jelli had a negative stigma about herself that Phatmama didn't need in her presence. All Jelli's negativity would have done was cloud her thoughts and made her have to whip her ass.

"Here, Phatmama!" Tata handed Phatmama the Backwoods. "You been quiet over here this whole time. Where your head at, *mami*? Talk to me."

Phatmama accepted the hemp from her boss. "I'm still a little shook up about what happened earlier. Shit, bitch almost lost her life. I'm still trying to wrap my head around what the fuck is going on and who the fuck trying to kill me."

Tata picked up on how Phatmama used the word "me" instead of "us" when she talked about getting killed, but she held her tongue for a second time that day.

Phatmama wanted badly to tell Tata what was going on, but she held her confession. She knew a storm was brewing, and she would have to alert her friends soon so they could avoid the hail of bullets gearing up to come their way.

Jibril Williams

CHAPTER 3

"Fuck! Oh, shit! I'm cumming, Diego! Ooh, baby, ooh! Fuck! You betta not stop!" Ski screamed, trying to maneuver her way out of the position Diego had her body balled up in.

Diego was serving Ski with them long, strong thrusts, the kind where he pulled out to the tip and then slammed into her pelvis. Diego stared down at his dick being gobbled up by Ski's tight pussy. Thick creaminess started to formulate around Diego's meat every time he sank deep into Ski.

"Yes, bae! Beat this pussy, bae!"

Ski was a straight-up bad chick, look-wise. This supa-thick chick was only sixteen, yet had the body and assets of a woman who was twenty-five. And just from looking, he could not tell she was at a tender, young age. That's why Diego had her once he laid eyes on the 5'5", Destiny Moore, Latino-looking beauty. He had to have her. The way she looked at Diego with those hazel eyes was breathtaking. Ski's body looked like someone carved her frame by hand with her small waist, flat stomach, and perky 36 DD breasts. Anyone who thought Tip on *Love & Hip Hop Miami* had an ass on her hadn't seen shit until they'd seen Ski's ass. Ski was a trophy, hands down. But just like most young girls who grew up in the hood, she learned through sex and exploring her sexuality that it could get her the finer things in life. Ski wasn't different than any other young female in the hood. Ski was a gold digger who didn't fuck with broke niggas. This was another reason she hooked up with Diego.

Diego zeroed in on Ski's pink folds and smashed his strokes as his nuts slapped against Ski's asshole, sounding off with a flapping sound. Sweat glistened and dripped from Diego's body onto Ski. The couple had been going at it for the last forty minutes. Ski loved it when Diego fucked her long and hard with so much passion. She considered the times like these as them making love, but at the moment, that was far from the truth. Diego was taking his frustrations out on Ski's sixteen-year-old pussy. His mind was burdened with the failed hit at the Harmony Cemetery, so cumming was far from his mind. Ski had reached her pleasure peak three times already and was fast approaching a fourth. Diego bit down on his bottom lip and hammered away in Ski's gushy love box. His nuts continued to fall against Ski's brown hole.

"Oh! Bae, yes, yes, yes. Gimme that dick," Ski cried out in pleasure.

Diego's pounding caused Ski's pretty hazel eyes to roll into the back of her head. Diego was slamming pipe at different angles, taking a piece out of a porn flick. Ski wetted two of her fingers by placing them in her mouth. She used those wet fingers to viciously rub her phat clit, bringing her fourth orgasm to a head. "Ooh, Diego! I'm cumming again!" Ski screamed out.

Diego was on a long ride on Ski, but he was at his peak. Seeing Ski's creamy juices coating his shaft brought him to an eruption. His abs flexed hard and his nut sack drew up. He let one of Ski's legs fall from his shoulders, unleashing a wild roar. "Argh! Argh!" Diego snatched his dick out of Ski, which caused her to grab ahold of his glistening dick and jack his load all over her stomach. Ski rubbed Diego's mushroom-shaped head in his juices, making his dick twitch and jump in Ski's hand in the process.

Ski grabbed Diego's dick at its base and squeezed it tightly, milking him, bringing an M&M sized glob of nut out of the head of Diego's meat. She swiped a manicured thumb across the head, catching the last drop of Diego. She placed her thumb in her mouth along with the treat attached to it. "Mmm, bae, I love your taste," Ski said in her Cardi-B voice.

Diego was speechless as he held himself in a push-up position overtop of Ski, breathing hard, trying to collect his breath. He collapsed right next to Ski on his back. Diego retrieved a Newport from the nightstand while Ski got up to go clean herself of the sex pasted on her stomach. Diego watched the sway of Ski's hips and how her booty cheeks banged together as she walked to the bathroom.

Lighting up the stick of nicotine, Diego took a pull and let out a cloud of smoke. His belle came back, jumped into bed with him, and laid her head on his chest.

Diego's thoughts were heavy. He knew he had probably fucked up the only chance he had at filling Rocco's position in his Uncle

Cain's organization. Cain was going to go ape-shit when he found out Diego had located the bitch who robbed and killed his cousin Rocco and failed to give him a call to inform Cain he had located the bitch.

Diego didn't expect the bitch and her friends to clap back the way they did. Shit, he wasn't expecting them to be strapped. He sent some of his flunkies – who were only under him in hopes of getting close to Cain – to go to the cemetery and kidnap the bitch, but shit went wrong. His flunkies were bagged and tagged, and he still didn't have the bitch who murdered his cousin.

Cain and Fate had to make an emergency trip out of town. Cain entrusted Diego to hold shit down for a few days. Diego shook his head. He couldn't fathom how he was going to begin to explain his fuck-up to Cain. The bitch at the cemetery had not only robbed them, but she had spilled family blood. She hit them for all Rocco's money and ten bricks of heroin that belonged to Cain.

Cain had placed Diego on a dummy mission. He knew how badly Diego wanted to step up and eat off a bigger plate and fulfill the empty slot his cousin once held. Cain sent Diego off with a picture of Rocco's killer, which he obtained from security footage. Cain instructed Diego that if he wanted to occupy Rocco's position, he first had to locate Rocco's killer in the picture. Diego knew it was impossible to do, but the gangster God in the sky favored him. Diego stumbled across his cousin's killer at his girl Ski's uncle's funeral.

Cain can't be mad at me, Diego thought to himself. *Cain left me in charge, and I made an executive decision.* Diego knew he could get shit under control. All he had to do was locate the bitch again. But first he needed to find out who the bitch and her peoples were before Cain and Fate made it back from out of town.

"Aye, bae, you up?" Diego asked, letting out another cloud of smoke.

"Yeah, baby," Ski said in her sleepy voice. Her uncle Rico's funeral was stressful and had left her feeling exhausted. She was happy Diego had some business to handle after the funeral and couldn't escort her to Harmony Cemetery to see Rico laid to rest. Ski's mom, Tina, had already told them she wasn't going to the cemetery, so Diego had Tina drop Ski off at his apartment while he went to Harmony

Cemetery to watch his flunkies kidnap his cousin's killer.

"The lady at Rico's funeral that we sat behind, you know, the big-boned chick that wore the dark Gucci shades. Who is she?"

Ski searched her mind tor the memory. "You talking about Phatmama. That's my Aunt Tata's best friend. They did time in the Feds together. That's where they became tight at. Why you wanna know about her?" Ski questioned. She lifted her head from Diego's chest and looked him in his eyes.

"It's nothing, bae, she just looked familiar, like I've seen her somewhere before," Diego said, reaching over and flicking ashes in a nearby ashtray.

There were some things Ski wanted to tell Diego concerning what she knew about Rico's death and what involvement her aunt and Phatmama had in it, but now that Diego inquired about Phatmama, her intuition told her not to. Ski kissed Diego on the chest and let out a sigh.

Diego ran his fingers through Ski's silky mane and kissed her on the top at her head. The wheels of Diego's mind started to turn in a devious manner. Now that he had the information that he need to locate Phatmama, he could handle his business and claim Rocco's position.

Diego knew where Tata lived, and Tata would lead him straight to Phatmama. This revelation made Diego smile. Finding Phatmama was going to be a G move for him.

CHAPTER 4

The big 3-0 was a poverty-stricken neighborhood in the Northeast, Washington, D.C. area that was infested with drug dealers and those who were addicted to the drugs. This is where the D.C.B. took up home base.

Whip eased his Charger in front of a rundown trap house. The drug traffic was bare to none. This was a sure sign that the work Whip had copped and put out in the trap house was some garbage, resulting in him not going to make a profit. It was turning out to be harder than he thought to build this new Blood line in D.C.

Whip put the car in park and looked over at Racks. She had been withdrawn ever since they left the group of killer babes. Whip didn't understand why Racks was caught on fucking with them reckless-ass bitches. He could respect that she wanted to pay her debt to them for saving her life, and she had done this at the cemetery. But right now, he needed Racks to get her head right.

"You still trippin' on that bullshit with them hoes?" Whip inquired.

Racks let out a sigh and ran her hands across her face. "I'm not trippin', Whip. It's just when muthafuckas save your ass from being in a tight jam, you got to be forever grateful to them and I can't just leave them when the favor is returned to them. Same bitches that you were so quick to walk out on was there when I killed that Metropolitan Police. I wanted to be there for them to establish and solidify a bond between us," Racks said in disappointment as she watched a young woman make her way up the stairs to the trap house. The woman wore some jeans that were way too large for her frail body.

"You paid your debt to them bitches that day at the cemetery. Now let that shit go! And if you having any doubts about keeping the police killing under wraps, then we need to murder them bitches immediately, swiftly, and without mercy. Do you think you we need to handle them bitches?" Whip questioned, snatching Racks by the chin, making her look him in the eyes.

Whip's face was so close to hers, she could smell the weed stench on his breath. "Naw. I don't feel like we need to bring Tata and them any harm." Racks yanked her chin out of Whip's hand.

The action made Whip react. Racks was the little homie and Whip was the big homie, so in this Blood Nation, disrespect wouldn't be tolerated. With lightning speed, the palm of Whip's hand found its home on Racks' face. He pushed Racks' face against the Charger's passenger window and held it there as he spoke.

"Listen, Racks, I love you like my own li'l sista. But I will not tolerate any disrespect from my foot soldiers. We got other shit on our plate than to be worrying about some bitches we don't know nothing about," Whip spoke through clenched teeth.

Whip had his face even closer to Racks' face. She could feel his breath on her facial skin. She wanted to go for the cannon on her hip and get Whip off of her. However, in doing so, she knew she would've issued her own death warrant with the rest of the D.C. B.'s. Even if Racks wanted to kill Whip, she couldn't do it since Whip had brought her into the fold and turned her from prey to predator.

"I got'chu, Whip! I hear you!" Racks stated with her head still pressed against the Charger's glass.

Whip stared at Racks just to make sure that she had an understanding. Once that was established, Whip exited the car and made his way inside the trap house. Racks followed, feeling fucked up from what Whip had just put down on her.

"What it do, Blood!" Whip said when he stepped into the trap house, where members of his Blood Family occupied the dingy and dimly lit living room. Empty bottles of E&J and roaches littered the floor. The air in the room was stale and a funk lingered in the air.

"Suu Wuu!" the three homies announced in sync, greeting their OG, throwing up a Blood sign with their fingers.

"Aye, Whip, this dope is some cold garbage. I damn near got to make the fiends cop it. When you gave us the package this morning, I was hoping to have this trap jumping hard like they did in *Traphouse Kings* by Hood Rich." Boot said with a disappointed look on his face. "We opened the trap at 5 this morning. It's now 10 p.m. and we only brought in $1,000. This shit ain't even worth the hassle," Boot complained.

Boot was one of Whip's most loyal comrades. There was nothing on this God green Earth that Boot wouldn't do for Whip. Boot was second in command in the D.C.B.'s. They had been trying for the longest to get the big homies out on the West Coast to give them the blessing to start their own line of Bloods. Now that they got the blessing, they needed to keep their Blood line in existence.

Boot was a straight grimy-ass nigga that only Whip could appreciate. Boot was cut up like an action figure, but never indulged in working out a day in his life. His graffiti-looking tattoos had his body marked up like the subways in Harlem. He stood 5'9" with a chipped tooth and a piece of missing bottom lip, which he lost in a night club brawl a few years ago. It made him look like the type of nigga you didn't want to fuck with. Boot's black beady eyes told a story that ended with death and mayhem. Boot was a brown-skinned, bald-headed nigga that rocked a goatee that made him look older than twenty-four. Even though he was two years younger than Whip, his body count was countless.

"I could tell by the traffic when I pulled up that product wasn't hittin' on shit," Whip said, sitting down on the futon and knocking a roach onto the floor.

"Blood, we need a lick, fast, and in a muthafuckin' hurry. There's some lame-ass niggas that got a good operation jumping off out M.D. in the front of that carry-out, Johnny Boys. We can hit them and come up real quick," Boot informed Whip.

"Shit, a lick is cool. But how long you think we going to eat off that lick? What we need is a plug. One lick ain't gonna feed and build our organization. We got twenty Bloods under our command that's starving. We got to get a plug ASAP." Whip paused to think for a minute. "This what you do. Take $2,500 and slide up on them niggas out Johnny Boys. Be polite and ask them niggas for a play, meaning give us a deal for the $2,500, and in return, we'll do straight business with them in the future. But if they shit on us, take it all! Got it?"

Boot wasn't really feeling what Whip was saying. He would rather take them niggas' shit and keep on mobbing. He understood clearly what Whip was trying to initiate. Whip wanted to establish good business ties and didn't want the D.C.B.'s name to be muddied up, but Boot felt the family was starving and it was time to smash the gas and get to the bag.

"Where the fuck that young dope head at that just came in here?" Whip asked, looking around the room for answers.

Boot had a smirk on his face, and the other young homies dropped their eyes to the dirty carpet. Whip got off the futon and made his way to the back of the house.

The farther he moved down the hall, the more clearly he could make out the moans and grunts coming from the backroom.

Whip pushed the door open, only to find one of the li'l homies, Ink, with the dope fiend. She had her dingy, two sizes too big jeans down to the floor. The fiend had her ankles in a choke hold while the nigga Ink stood behind her, feeding her asshole nothing but wood. The air in the small stuffy room changed as the door opened, alerting Ink that someone had entered the room.

"Shit!" Ink snatched his dick out the girl's brown hole, horrified to see Whip standing there with an insulted look on his face. "Wassup, Blood?" Ink saluted Whip.

"Hard lesson!" Whip shot back at Ink. "Need to see ya in the front room. Bring that bitch wit'cha," Whip stated, closing the door behind him."

Ink entered the living room, where Whip waited for him. Ink's stomach bubbled from nervousness. The dope fiend scratched at her arms. The small pus-like sores on her arms told that she preferred to push her poison in her veins instead of snorting it. The living room was so quiet that you could hear the roaches crawling over the carpet.

"Shawty, is this nigga right here your man?" Whip asked, pointing towards Ink.

With snot running down her nose, the dope fiend shook her head from side to side. You could tell that the young girl was a cutie until she got hooked on drugs.

"So my man here has paid you for the sexual favor I seen you performing for him in the back room?"

The girl hesitated. She was embarrassed by Whip's line of questioning, but she nodded her head up and down shamefully.

"Hold up!" Ink yelled, trying to interject, but was cut short when Whip pointed a 50 caliber Desert Eagle in his face. Ink swallowed his words.

"How did this nigga pay you for your service?" Whip continued to question the girl.

Seeing Whip's big-ass gun had this girl frightened shitless. She shifted her weight from one leg to the other.

"Go ahead. No one is going to hurt you," Whip assured her.

She dug a crusty hand into her back pocket and came out with a ten dollar bag of heroin, which Whip was very familiar with. Whip had bagged the dope up in small red zips, which was the same bag the girl held out in her hand.

A savage look came into Whip's eyes. The look was more menacing through the bifocal lenses he wore. "You telling me that our Blood line is starving and the same product we trying to use to feed this family with, you're tricking it off on some dope fiend bitch!" Whip's voice bellowed throughout the trap house.

"Big homie, it's only a $10.00 bag of dope," Ink stated, trying to rationalize with Whip.

"I don't give a fuck if it was a one dollar! No one gave you permission to misuse it! That bag of dope belongs to every member under D.C.B.'s umbrella! Did Boot give you permission to misuse this dope?"

Ink's eyes shot to Boot, who sat in a chair next to the window. Boot had an evil glare in his eye. Ink knew that Boot gave him permission to use the $10.00 bag, but he wouldn't dare rat Boot out. Ink knew whatever Whip had for him, Boot's punishment was going to be ten times worse if he ratted Boot out.

"Naw, fam. Boot ain't gimme no permission," Ink stuttered.

"Well, nigga, you in violation. Drop your pants," Whip ordered.

"Come on, Whip. Don't do this to me, Blood."

"Nigga, drop your pants or I'll drop your ass right here!" Whip said, jacking a rhino slug in the 50 Cal.

Ink hesitantly untied the string to his Polo sweatpants. His sweats fell around his Nike boots.

"Boxers too, nigga," Whip demanded.

Everyone in the room turned their heads from Ink's shriveled-up dick. Everyone except Boot. Boot had amazement in his eyes.

"Now you wanted to get your dick sucked. I'm gonna grant you that. Bitch, suck his dick," instructed Whip to the dope fiend.

The girl fell to her knees, quickly took Ink into her mouth, and started bobbing her head up and down.

Ink thought the big homie was just clowning him, so he relaxed and grew stiff as a board in the fiend's mouth. He even grabbed the back of the girl's head and started rocking back and forth in her mouth. Racks shook her head at Ink. The little respect she had for him was now out of the window. Ink's action had shown her just how weak he really was.

Once Whip saw Ink enjoying himself, he placed the Desert Eagle to the girl's head and ordered her to bite down as hard as she could on Ink's dick.

Ink quickly yanked his dick back from the girl's mouth.

"Nigga, put'cha dick back in her mouth!" Whip said as he pushed the barrel of his gun into Ink's right eye socket. Ink took a deep breath and did what he was told. Ink was now trembling as he placed his member back into the girl's mouth. Whip pointed the hand cannon back at the girl's head and ordered "Bite!"

The girl bit down hard on Ink's manhood. Her teeth sank into Ink's meat like those of a pit-bull.

"Arrrrrrrhhhhhhh!" Ink screamed.

The two other goons grabbed their dicks through their jeans. The thought of the pain that Ink had to be going through made them cringe and their manhoods shriveled up. Boot fell on the floor in laughter. He loved to see wild shit like he was witnessing at that moment.

The fiend's mouth filled up with blood before she released Ink from her mouth. Ink fell to the floor clutching his wounded penis. The fiend's teeth had sliced through the skin of Ink's penis, marking it with ugly gashes.

"Let this be a hard lesson to all of you. We don't trick off the family's money or product. We have an organization to build. That's our prime focus. If I catch anyone doing anything outside of that, then another hard lesson will be taught," Whip stated, making eye contact with everyone in the room. Once he was sure that his message was received, he tucked away his hand cannon and exited the trap house

CHAPTER 5

"It's good seeing you again, my friend," Weedy said, extending his hand to Cain and giving him a firm handshake. He acknowledge Cain's bodyguard with a slight head nod, which Fate returned.

"Likewise. But what brings about this emergency meeting?" Cain said, scanning the room and giving a greeting head nod to Weedy's bodyguard Flex. Cain let Weedy's hand go and adjusted his Tom Ford suit jacket. He tugged at the cuffs of his Tom Ford shirt sleeves that poked out the sleeve of his jacket. The cream-colored suit was tailor-fitted. Cain looked as though he was a high class business man instead of a drug dealer.

"We will get to that soon. What about patience? There's none of that anymore in this game we play. Everyone's in a rush, and that's how we miss things, by not being patient," Weedy said, dropping an old jewel on Cain.

Cain took what Weedy spoke with respect and settled down. "Can I get you a drink? Perhaps a glass of Cuvee Leonie Cognac?"

"Sure, why not?" Cain stated. He was honored that Weedy offered the expensive drink. Something special had to be in store because a bottle of Cuvee Leonie Cognac easily ran $150,000 a bottle. Since Weedy called for a meeting on such short notice, Cain wasn't going to feel guilty about drinking Weedy's expensive liquor.

Cain took a seat in front of Weedy's office desk and Fate took post next to his boss' chair. Weedy came back with a single bottle of Harvet 1858 Cuvee Leonie along with two shot glasses. Weedy took a seat behind his desk and Flex positioned himself behind him.

Weedy filled both shot glasses and pushed a glass of the exclusive cognac towards Cain. Weedy removed a cigar box from his desk drawer and retrieved a Cuban cigar, clipping the end and lighting it.

Cain wasn't a fool. He knew that Weedy was prolonging for a reason, and this fact alone made Cain uncomfortable. Cain took Weedy's appearance in. The tan Giorgio Armani suit fit Weedy immaculately. His Almond Joy-colored skin blended in well with the color of his suit he wore. Even though Weedy was fifty-two years old, he still carried his 5'9" frame with youth. Weedy was a man that didn't eat meat and didn't indulge in eating junk food. These habits contributed to his looking lean and fit. Weedy's greenish eyes held a seriousness within them and a glare that said, "I've seen it all: the good, the bad, and the ugly."

Cain and Weedy had encountered each other in Atlantic City, NJ in a hotel parking lot. Two jack boys from the NJ area were playing the casinos in Atlantic City for an easy come-up. From a distance, the goons watched Weedy do his thing on the craps table. It seemed that was Weedy's lucky night as the two pairs of eyes watched him. Cain was at the craps table too, piggybacking off of Weedy's lucky hand. Cain was placing side bets with every number that Weedy threw. Cain could see that Weedy had the attributes of a boss, a man that was deep in the underworld. Cain was on a mission to find a plug. That was his purpose in Atlantic City. He was supposed to be meeting a potential plug, but for some reason, the plug that he was supposed to meet never showed up.

Weedy won quite a bit of the casino's money that night. When he went to cash his chips in, adding fifteen racks to his already fat bankroll, Weedy was ready to call it a night and end his night in some high-priced pussy.

Weedy made his way out of the casino and gave the parking valet his ticket to fetch his car. The two goons that were watching him followed and Cain, being the observant man that he was, followed the goons.

Weedy was a little tipsy as the valet attendant pulled Weedy's Benz around front. Weedy hopped in his luxury ride and pulled out, making a right turn into an underground hotel parking lot on the Atlantic boardwalk. Weedy parked his whip close to the elevator. When he was exiting his car, a gray Malibu pulled up on his Benz, quickly boxing him in. Two hooded figures hopped out of the Malibu. One pointed his .38 special at Weedy while the other on approached him with a P89 Ruger at his side.

The jack boy opened his door, dragged Weedy out of his Benz, and started going through his pockets, searching for the fifteen racks Weedy won at the casino. The robber pocketed all of Weedy's money and then started removing his jewelry. Weedy cursed under his breath for leaving his gun in the trunk.

Out of nowhere, gunshots rang out. The .38 special handler's head exploded. The goon that was stripping Weedy of his jewelry caught a slug to the neck. He fell to the pavement clutching this neck, trying to stop himself from bleeding out. Cain walked out of the shadows between two parked trucks, holding his own P89 Ruger.

That night, a friendship was born, and Weedy became the plug for Cain. But now Cain sat in front of Weedy's desk and he asked himself if he could continue to trust Weedy.

"So you summon me all the way from D.C. to Connecticut just so we could have a drink?" Cain questioned, finally breaking the silence.

Weedy knocked back a drink and Cain followed suit. Weedy refilled their glasses, took another pull of his Cuban cigar, and stared at Cain. Cain downed his second shot of cognac without breaking eye contact with his friend and connect.

"Business been good with you, Cain. You always been on time with your payments and at times you paid up front," Weedy finally spoke. Cain nodded his head up and down. "But it's time that you join my ranks and work with me and relinquish to the Canadian Mob," Weedy stated.

Cain closed his eyes tightly and shook his head at Weedy's request.

Weedy let out a deep sigh from Cain's gesture. "I don't get it, Cain. I'm offering you a lifetime opportunity. Why won't you take it? You would be tripling the profit that you are making now."

"We been through this already before, Weedy!" Cain began to raise his voice. "I DON'T WORK FOR NO FUCKIN' BODY. I'M MY OWN FUCKIN' BOSS!"

"Listen, my friend. It's not about being a boss at this moment, because you're always going to be a boss in your own right. But it's about the green pieces of paper with them slave masters on them."

"But joining your ranks means I'll be giving up my power, and having my own power is priceless. You can't place a price on being able to move on your own accordance. I didn't get this far in the game being a fool. So tell me, why the hell you trying so hard to get me to join forces with you? What's really on your mind, Weedy?" Cain

Asked.

The greenness in Weedy's eyes turned a shade darker. He set the cigar in a crystal ashtray, steepled his fingers together, and rested his elbows on his desk. "The family back home is under new management. They want the whole fuckin' East Coast, from Canada to Florida."

What Weedy just revealed left silence in the room. Cain swallowed hard and sat up straight up in his chair.

"What the fuck the new management got to do with me and my city? They can run their pipeline from Canada to Miami as long as they run that bitch around D.C. I'm not giving up my city, Weedy." Spit spritzed out of Cain's mouth on to Weedy's desk. Flex step forward as well as Fate. Both Cain and Weedy waved their respective bodyguards off.

"Cain, I been holding the Canadian Mob at bay for months. They have already begun to gain some traction with this takeover. They already occupy every major city from New Heaven to Maryland. Muthafuckas is letting the Canadian Mob buy their cities. The Mob is allowing them to keep running business as is, but just under the Canadian Mob management. Listen, Cain, D.C. is next on the list," Weedy proclaimed, getting a little agitated with Cain's stubbornness.

"You might have given your city up without a fight, but not me, Weedy. For mines, I'm willing to shed blood for it," Cain stated sternly, pulling a pack of Newports from his Tom Ford jacket. He lit one of the cancer sticks and inhaled deeply.

"Fuck, Cain! What you are not comprehending is that your face will still be the face of D.C."

"I understand that clearly, but what's hard for me to comprehend is me doing all the work and handing over all the money from that hard work to the Canadian Mob and only keeping a small percentage for myself. Be honest, Weedy, where the fuck they do that at?" Cain asked, filling his glass with more cognac.

Weedy grabbed his cigar out he ashtray and puffed the Cuban until the cherry glowed red on the end. "Well, at least let them buy out," Weedy said through clouds of smoke.

Cain laughed at Weedy's comment. "My city is not for sale."

"Five million is the price they are offering, and they are only entertaining this price on the strength of me. The other cities that didn't take the million dollars the Mob was offering, the Mob just muscled their way in."

"Tell them cold dick muthafuckas to keep their money and stay the fuck out my city unless I invite them," Cain stated, downing his drink. But mentally, Cain couldn't deny the thought of getting that five million. Greed had a way of doing that to a man.

Cain stood to his feet. Weedy held his hand up, signaling for Cain to hold fast.

"There's something else," Weedy said.

Cain sighed. He knew what was coming.

"I was ordered to cut the plug with you if I couldn't formulate some type of agreement with you that will benefit both parties," Weedy stated bluntly.

Cain's blood began to boil and a layer of sweat began to coat his forehead. Cain fought to maintain his composure. "How much time I got?" Cain questioned.

"About, give or take, ninety days," Weedy admitted.

"Good. Double the shipment until then and in ninety days, I'll let you know what it is," Cain said, smashing his Newport out in the ashtray.

Weedy looked at Cain with a concerned look in his eyes. Over the years, Weedy had formulated a love for Cain like a brother, but Cain had to know that he couldn't go against the Canadian Mob.

Cain sensed what Weedy was thinking. "What's understood doesn't need to be addressed," Cain said.

Weedy nodded in agreement. Weedy rose to his feet and made his way around his desk to embrace Cain in a bear hug, which Cain returned.

"I will double the shipment, but promise me during those ninety days you will think long and hard about the five million offer. And always remember this, Cain: that city would never be yours, so if someone is ignorant enough to give you five million for a city that the government owns, then take it, because it was never yours from the beginning."

"I hear ya, Weedy," Cain said, understanding the jewel that Weedy just dropped on him.

The friends released their embrace and Cain made his way out of Weedy's office with heavy thoughts on his mind.

CHAPTER 6
Three days later

Rotating the nine black diamonds back and forth in the palm of her hand placed Tata in a state of awe, that's how beautiful the jewels were. Just having the diamonds in her possession made her feel powerful and sexy for some reason. Maybe because the worth of the nine precious stones was $360,000, $40,000 apiece.

The way the room lights ricocheted and danced off the diamonds brought the stones to life, making Tata's pussy moist in the process. Ever since she and the Red Bottom Clique pulled the ZALES heist and the diamonds landed in their possession, this had been Tata's morning ritual, pulling the precious diamonds out and ogling them. Tata placed the beautiful stones back into the black velvet bag and drew the bag string, sealing the diamonds inside. She stash the bag inside a floor vent of her two bedroom apartment. After the Feds raided hers and Rico's house, she immediately went out and rented a low-key apartment out of Oak Crest Towers in Capitol Heights off of Brooks Drive.

Tata loved her house, but she would never feel comfortable and safe there after the Feds ransacked it. She was taking no chances, thinking that the Feds may have planted listening devices in her house. She called a realtor and placed the house on the market.

Tata started placing the stacks of money on her king-sized bed in three Victoria's Secret Shopping bags. She packed them with a hundred thousand apiece. She was giving Phatmama, Jelli, and Zoey their cut of the money that they had gotten from killing and robbing Rico. The $400,000 was what the group needed. They had $365,000 in the stash from the jewels that she sold to Rau'f from the McCormick & Smit job that Rico had pulled. Tata still had the merchandise from the Zales heist. She was going to call Rau'f soon and dump the jewels off on him for a good price, but she wasn't ready to come up off the black diamonds just yet.

Tata looked at her peach-colored Cartier watch and checked the time. It was 10:45 a.m. Her team was supposed to be there at 10:15 a.m. "What the fuck?" Tata said in concern to herself. She started searching for her phone to give Phatmama a text to see what the holdup was. Phatmama had told her that morning that she had something to tell her. Tata was hoping that it wasn't going to be some bullshit like she wasn't going to help pull the new lick off with them because she wanted to change her life because of the shootout they had at the cemetery.

Before she could send Phatmama a text, there was a knock at the door. Tata grabbed a pair of gray sweatpants with the word PINK plastered across the back of them. The sweatpants hugged her curves firmly. She then pulled a white wife beater over her perky B-cups and grabbed Rico's chrome fo'-fifth with the red crushed diamond handle along with the money and went to answer the door. Tata dropped the Victoria's Secret bags on the living room table and went and peeped through the peephole. Phatmama and Zoey stared back at her. Tata opened the door, clutching the fo'-fifth.

"Bitch, what took your ass so long?" Tata complained.

"Buenos dias to you, mami," Phatmama said, kissing Tata on the cheek. "I had to go pick up Zoey and Billie. Then Zoey's greedy ass wouldn't stop crying about her ass was hungry until I stopped past Horace & Dickies Fish Shack to get her a fish platter."

Tata didn't hear anything else Phatmama was saying after she mentioned that she had to pick up Billie. Bringing Billie to her house had Tata confused, and Zoey read it on Tata's face.

"I felt the same way, but just hear a bitch out. Shit about to get deeper than rap. And damn, you look sexy in them sweats clutching that four pound," Zoey said, handing Tata a fish platter from Horace & Dickies.

"Heeey, Tata!" Billie spoke in her southern drawl, bringing up the rear.

Tata didn't have anything against Billie or white people in particular, but what she didn't like was those white bitches that had a mysterious craving for that black dick, and Billie definitely had a hoggish appetite for black men.

"What it do, Billie?" Tata stated dryly, closing the door behind Billie and checking her out.

Billie was a white chick that was built like a sister below the waist.

She had a round juicy booty and thick hips and thighs to accommodate her pretty face. And the fact that Billie could dress enhanced her beauty. The Dolce & Gabbana romper was fitting her right. Her backside jiggled uncontrollably as she walked, which made Tata roll her eyes. Zoey giggled at Tata's gesture. The black Red Bottoms Billie wore had her standing a little taller than Tata. Billie was a perfect 9, but Tata wouldn't admit that though. Tata wasn't a hater; she just hated when white women didn't date in their race. For a minute Tata thought she was being a hypocrite because she was Puerto Rican and all she dated was black men.

"What's good, Phatmama?" Tata said, placing the fish platter on the island. She removed a piece of grilled salmon from the tray and bit into it.

"I prefer to wait until Jelli gets here. I see that she's late also. But until she gets here, let's smoke something." Phatmama pulled out an already-rolled Garcia Vega from her clutch.

Tata nodded her head up and down in agreement. "Ashtray over there on the remote stand at the end of the sofa," Tata instructed.

Zoey found a home in the tan recliner and Billie sat next to Phatmama on the matching sofa. Once Phatmama blazed the sour diesel and the Vega got to burning good, Tata's curiosity got the best of her. She couldn't wait until Jelli got there. She had to know why Phatmama brought Billie to her crib.

"I don't mean no disrespect, Phatmama, but why you bring Billie here?" Tata bluntly questioned her best friend.

"I knew your ass couldn't wait until Jelli got here. But since you're so damn impatient…" Phatmama hit the Vega one good time before she passed it to Billie and continued to talk. "I know who tried to kill us," Phatmama said, letting out a cloud of smoke.

Tata's heart thumped heard in her chest. She could barely get the word out her mouth. "Who?"

"Well, I think it's a nigga named Cain," Phatmama replied.

"Cain? Why would this nigga want to kill us?" Tata questioned with her face scrunched up.

Phatmama was silent for a few seconds before she answered Tata. "A few months ago, I met this dude named Rocco at the club. We traded numbers and hooked up. Just to keep shit short and sweet, me and Billie hit him for a check and murdered his ass."

The revelations left Tata's mouth wide open. She darted her eyes back and forth between Phatmama and Billie.

"Before you say anything, let me continue," Phatmama said. "That day at the cemetery when that nigga stood over me with his banga, he stated, 'This is fo' Rocco' before Racks knocked a chunk out his dome. The word on the streets is Rocco was Cain's cousin. Cain is supposed to be the nigga in the city, I mean a real boss type nigga," Phatmama said, looking at Tata.

"I told you this shit deeper than rap," Zoey said with a chuckle.

Tata rolled her eyes at Zoey's comment. "Okay, do you know for sure if it's Cain that wants you dead?" Tata asked. She was pissed that Phatmama had done some dumb-ass shit like this, but now wasn't the time to express it.

"I'm 90% sure, Tata. Rocco talked a lot about how his big cousin Cain had the city on smash. When I did my homework on Rocco, I found out that indeed Cain was the man to be connected to in this city, and Rocco was moving some major weight for him."

Tata raked her French manicure over her face. She knew if the info Phatmama had just given her was halfway accurate, then the Red Bottom Squad was in some deep shit. Tata knew it took an army to fight with a well-established muthafucka like Cain, but she refused to leave Phatmama in a fucked up predicament.

"If you think we going to be able to take on Cain, then we gotta be smart about it. And we got to run the bag up if we are going to war with Cain," Tata stated. All heads in the room nodded up and down in agreement.

"There's another reason why I brought Billie to this meeting," Phatmama stated.

"Why?" Tata and Zoey asked in sync.

Zoey got out the recliner and got the burning Vega from Billie. Tata took another bite of her salmon. Phatmama hesitated.

"I want to bring Billie on board with the Clique."

"Hell no!" Tata protested.

"Why not? She got military training. She served in the same

platoon that I did in the Army and we can trust her."

"How you know that we can trust her?" Tata asked Phatmama, but she had her eyes on Billie the hold time.

Before Phatmama could speak up on her friend's behalf, Billie spoke up. "Look, Tata, I know you don't know me, nor do you know my struggle."

"Yeah, you right, and?" Tata said, cutting Billie off.

"But trust me, my background probably as real as yours. You see this pale skin and think I'm just another cracker that wants to be black, but my struggle is real. The shit that I done been through helps me relate to the black race. Under pressure, I don't wither or fold. I live under the principle 'Loose Lips Sink Ships' and 12 don't know shit unless a bitch tells them."

"But no one in this room wants to take that chance with you," Zoey chimed in.

"Man, fuck that, Billie is already with us whether you like it or not. Remember, she helped smash Rocco, and if Cain wants me dead, then he sure wants her dead too, and I'm not going to let shit happen to Billie," Phatmama stated firmly.

Tata heard the profoundness in Phatmama's voice and an idea came to her. "Phatmama, when you robbed Rocco, I know there was some work. Please tell me that you grabbed it and that you still have it?" Tata's phone notified her that she had a text.

"I got every gram of the work and the money that came with it," Phatmama replied.

"Good. We going to need it," Tata stated, reading the text from Jelli telling her she was going to be late.

"So Billie in, right?" Phatmama asked, getting back on topic.

Tata could see that Phatmama was grounded in her loyalty to Billie, and she could understand loyalty between two individuals. Tata knew they could use some new members in the Clique and if Billie was really about that life, then she could be a great fit, but she was going to use this opportunity as leverage to get what she wanted also.

"Phat, shit ain't official yet, but Billie is your responsibility until further notice. Whatever she does, it falls on you." Tata paused, letting what she just stated sink in with Phatmama and Billie. Phatmama wiped the excess oil from her nose and nodded her head up and down. "Please don't let this decision come back to haunt Red Bottom Squad."

"I promise it won't," Phatmama confirmed.

With that being said, Tata sent a text out on her phone.

CHAPTER 7

Jelli's head had a nice slow rhythm to it as it went up and down on Cain's meat pop. She made loud slurping sounds as she breathed through her nostrils and intensely worked her jaw muscles.

Cain stood in his kitchen clad in a black silk Prada robe with matching silk Prada boxers around his ankles. Cain watched Jelli take him whole in her mouth. Jelli pulled and popped the dick out of her mouth, viciously jacking it a few times before she placed it back into her wet mouth and continued to make love to Cain's dick with her tongue, mouth, and lips.

"Ummmmmm! I love this dick," Jelli spoke with mouth full of meat.

"And this dick loves you," Cain said, stuttering.

When Jelli came downstairs this morning with the intention to make herself some toast before heading out the door for the meeting with her girls, she found Cain in the kitchen cooking breakfast, looking handsomer than a muthafucka. Seeing his dick print bounce up against the silk fabric made her mouth water for him. Cain's brown skin and 6'2" frame had Jelli head over heels about him. When Cain's chestnut-colored eyes met hers, it made her suck harder on his nine inches of loveliness. Jelli sucked her lover's meat pop like a vacuum - Black & Decker, that is, like it setting was on low. She held him by the base and started licking all over the dick, getting it sloppy wet. Cain's mushroom-shaped head was the sensitive part of him and every time she flicked her tongue over it, his dick twitched in her grip.

Jelli's head game was on point. Cain tried his best to keep his moans from spilling out of his mouth, but he failed horribly. "Aye, bae, damn. Mmm, hold up, Jelli."

Cain tried to pull out of Jelli's mouth, but she wasn't having it. Jelli had his whole nine inches juicy and slippery. She made sure her lips, mouth, and face stayed wet. Pushing her lips tighter, she slurped his dick into her. Jelli then brought her lips up to the head of Cain's dick. She could tell he was on the verge of cumming. Jelli rolled her wet lips up and down him while she pressed her tongue on the underside of his big ole dick. The act made Cain's dick erupt like a volcano, which made Jelli shove Cain meat back into her mouth and suck and milk him dry. She made sure she left him empty.

Jelli got off her knees and walked over to the sink, where she spit Cain's babies out and washed her mouth, using the faucet water. Cain watched Jelli as he breathed hard, trying to regain his composure. The way that Jelli's black Robin jeans hugged her big round booty made Cain's dick jump. The way that she stood pigeon toed in her fire engine Giuseppe Zanetti stilettos had her looking sexier than any woman that he had laid eyes on. Jelli and Cain had grown close over the last year. There was no doubt in his mind that she was the one for him. He was ready to take the relationship to the next level. Cain loved everything about Jelli.

"Damn, you just going to spit a nigga's babies out like that?" Cain said with a chuckle as he pulled his boxers back up around his waist.

"Nigga, I'm not swallowing no babies or taking a dick in the dookie chute unless a nigga gonna upgrade me and put a ring on it," Jelli said seriously, patting her lips dry with a paper towel.

"Oh, that's all a nigga got to do to put all this meat in that big ole butt of yours?" Cain said, walking over to Jelli and wrapping his arms around her.

"Yup. I got to save something for my hubby. I can't just give you all of me without bearing your last name," Jelli retorted playfully. She and Cain made eye contact. She loved Cain on all levels. Jelli never had a man to shower her with and love her the way that Cain did. She was mentally fucked up about this man that held her in his arms.

"You keep talking like that, you might get that ring."

"Yeah right, I'll believe it when I see it. And you should know better than to play with a woman like that," Jelli said, kissing Cain on the lips and pushing herself out of his arms.

"Hold up, baby, where you going? Let's take it to the bedroom for round two." Cain tried to grab ahold of Jelli, but she wiggled away from him.

"Noooooo, Cain, I got to meet up with my girls, and I'm already late," Jelli said, opening her clutch that was on the kitchen table and retrieving a pack of Big Red gum and her phone. She popped a stick of gum in her mouth and sent a quick text to Tata telling her that she was going to be late.

"Come on, baby, let a nigga get a quickie before you go," Cain begged.

"Nope! I'll see you tonight," Jelli said and hit the door before Cain could convince her to oblige to his request.

Cain watched Jelli walk out the door. He bit down hard on his bottom lip, watching how Jelli's ass bounce in her jeans. He felt like he was truly blessed to have a dime like Jelli. Cain was ready to make Jelli his wifey. There was a lot that Jelli didn't know about him, and he had plans to reveal everything to her. He wasn't going to hold no punches. Cain already concluded that he was going to give the Canadian Mob D.C. for the five million, and with the money he already had saved, it was enough to retire from the game and live peacefully with Jelli and have a few kids.

Cain smiled at the thought of him having some little ones running around calling him Daddy. Cain's plan was to rack up as much money as he could before his ninety day grace period was up. Then he would be off with Jelli somewhere exotic.

*****

Jelli pulled up to Oak Crest Towers where Tata lived. She parked next to Tata's Infinity G37. Jelli placed some peach-flavored lip gloss on her lips, slid her Chanel shades over her eyes, and exited her Lexus RX 450 SUV. The red truck looked real sporty sitting on black 22 Ashanti Rims, a gift that Cain had given her two days ago. Her squad hadn't seen her new whip yet. Jelli patted her hip, making sure that her pink Glock was still secured there.

Jelli started making her way to Tata's apartment, strutting hard like a diva, her stilettos click-clacking against the pavement, her eyes hidden behind her dark shades Jelli caught a glimpse of Racks' dyke ass getting out of her beat up-ass Delta 88. Jelli knew that the car had seen better years.

Jelli rolled her eyes behind her lenses of her shades. *What the fuck this bum bitch doing here?* Jelli thought.

Jelli had already sent Tata a text and told her she was pulling up.

Tata lived on the first floor. By the time she was making it to Tata's apartment door, it opened and Tata greeted her.

"What it do, bitch!"

"Ain't shit, trying to run that bag up!" Jelli said, dapping Tata up with their signature handshake. The way they shook it up, you would had thought they were a part of some type of Blood gang or some shit.

Racks walked up the hall. Tata saw her coming and held the door open for her.

"I'm glad that you could make it, Racks," Tata stated and gave Racks a pound. "How you been doing?" Tata asked.

"Ain't too much going on with me, just enjoying the view," Racks stated, making the sly comment that she was enjoying the way Jelli's ass cheeks bounced in her jeans.

Jelli didn't know Racks had gained on her so quickly. She look over her shoulder at Racks.

"Dyke, don't play!" Jelli cautioned Racks about her slick-ass comment and for her to stay in her lane. "Tata, what the fuck she doing here?"

"We going to get into that in a minute. Just come in and have a seat."

Jelli walk in and the strong scent of the sour diesel hit her nose. "Damn, bitches smoke something, you bitches burn without me?" Jelli stated, scrunching her face up after seeing Billie sitting next to Phatmama.

Phatmama tossed Jelli a half ounce of sour diesel and a Garcia Vega. Jelli wasted no time twisting up. She had to get her mind right for the bullshit that she knew Tata was getting ready to drop on her. Seeing Billie and Racks there at the meeting was a sign that Tata had something up her sleeve.

"Bitch, you know that you dead-ass wrong. You know that we don't rock nothing but Red Bottoms in this squad," Zoey said with a little aggravation in her voice as she looked down at Jelli's stilettos.

"Damn, can't a bitch switch it up at times? You know a diva rockin' these joints like a boss bitch supposed to," Jelli countered, making an eye sweep of the room and seeing that Phatmama, Zoey, and Billie had on their trademark choice of shoe.

Tata shook her head like she wanted to say something, but she had bigger things on her plate, plus she thought the red Giuseppe Zanetti stilettos were bangin'.

"Before we get started, Jelli, the bag on the table belongs to you."

Jelli knew the bag held 100 bands. Tata already told her earlier what her take was going to be. She grabbed the bag and set it at her feet and fired up the Vega. She wasn't going to reveal what was in the bag because of the outsiders that were in the room and she didn't need them bitches in her business.

"As you can see, there are some new faces amongst us," Tata said this more for Jelli's benefit.

Jelli let out a cloud of smoke and listened.

"All of us in this room have a common denominator in between us." Tata paused. "And that's to secure that bag. And the only way to secure the bag is to put the bullshit to the side and unite forces and move as one while maintaining that heart of a savage. Phatmama wanted to bring Billie in the folds of our Red Bottom Clique and I want to bring Racks in as well." Tata looked into her team's eyes. She could see that Jelli was about to interject, but for some reason, she held what she had to say, so Tata kept talking. "I know I was against Billie joining us, but I trust Phatmama's judgement. I think we all do. So I'm asking for all to trust my judgment by accepting Racks into our circle."

Heads nodded up and down in the room.

"Hold up, Tata!" Racks spoke up. "I don't mind rockin' with your team on getting a bag. But until the casket drops, I'm a D.C. Blood," Racks stated sincerely, throwing up B's with her fingers. "And to be honest, Whip not going to let me rock with y'all on a level of trying to secure a bag when our own structure is suffering."

"I already took this under consideration. Me and Phatmama want you to set up a meeting with Whip. Could you do that?" Tata asked.

"Consider it done," Racks agreed.

"Okay, now with that being handled with all standing members of the Red Bottom Squad, show of hands, who's in agreement with Billie and Racks joining us?" Tata asked

Phatmama, Zoey, and Tata raised their hands. Jelli sat there with the tight face.

"The majority rules. Before I move forward, Billie, what do you have to bring to the table for this group?" Tata questioned.

Billie stood to her feet. "I own two small gun stores. I can bring to the table any type of weaponry and the ammunition that comes with it, but I also bring my undying loyalty," Billie confessed.

Damn! Tata thought to herself. She didn't know that Billie owned two gun stores. *That must be how Phatmama had been getting all the guns and bullets for the jobs we planned for Rico.* "We have a motto. If one rides, we all roll. If one hesitates, then we all motivate, and if one betrays...then God forgives. We don't. Do you accept?" Tata asked.

"It would be my pleasure," Billie replied in her Southern drawl.

"Embrace your sister," Tata informed the group. Tata didn't swear Racks in yet. She wanted to have the meeting with Whip before she did so.

The women embraced Billie. Tata went into her room and removed twenty-five bands out of her stash and returned to the front room. She gave Racks the money. "Give twenty bands to Whip. Tell him the Red Bottom squad is making a donation to the D.C.B.'s under the condition that he have a sit down with me and Phatmama. Keep five bands for yourself."

Racks was astounded. She wondered what these bitches were really into.

"Thanks, Tata."

"Don't trip. Just make the meeting happen with Whip."

"I will," Racks said.

"But look, we got some business to discuss. Give me a call with a date and time to meet with Whip," Tata said, dapping Racks up.

Tata let Racks out of her apartment and started plotting on the Red Bottom next heist.

CHAPTER 8
The next day

"Come on, Blood, play fair with a nigga. I'm trying to get it just like you," Boot said, shooting his spiral to the fake wannabe-ass goon.

"What part of the game you don't understand, playboy? I don't sell weight to a nigga that I don't know and if I did, I sure don't do no fuckin' deals, nigga!" The nigga Drake that ran the dope spot in front of Johnny Boys carryout was talking to Boot with his face all twisted while he rested his hand on his high point 380 that was on his waistline.

Boot was highly offended, but he keep his cool. The drug traffic that was coming in and out the establishment was unreal. There was no question that the spot was a gold mine. The drug traffic flowed in well with the carryout traffic.

"Just do this solid for me just this one time and I swear we both gonna get rich together," Boot pleaded.

"Bitch-ass Blood!"

With the speed of Money Mayweather, Boot chin checked the nigga Drake. While he was falling on his back pockets to take a concrete nap, Boot yanked the 10mm off this hip. Two members of the D.C.B.'s that were perpetrating like they were dope fiends up there fired on Drake's men. The Bloods had caught Drake's men slipping. They had been coming back and forth for the last two days acting like they were users and buying dope from Drake and his people. Pound had his 357 to the head of Drake's shooter. Pound relieved the goon of his 9mm. Taz cornered the pack boy who was in charge of making all transactions while Drake collected and held all the money. The trio had a smooth operation. Once the Drake boys made a thousand dollars, Drake would place a call to a red bone that lived in the corner house across the street. She would come out and retrieve the money from Drake and bring him another thousand dollar pack.

After Boot got all the money outta Drake's pockets and Taz got the dope from the pack boy, Boot gave the signal. Two members from D.C.B. jumped out of a black Ram 1500 and ran up to the house that the red bone live in. They kicked in the front door with one switch motion. You could hear the red bone chick scream from where Boot was standing. Moments later gunshots rang out and the two men with red bandanna's covering their face came out of the house with a pillow case. They jumped back in the Ram truck. One of the robbers threw up the Blood sign at Boot and the truck got ghost.

"Aye Blood, murk 'em," Boot said, hopping in the stolen white STS.

Taz wasted no time following orders. He dome checked the pack boy, knocking his noodles loose.

Pound smiled wickedly and Drake's shooter begged. "Come on, slim, you don't have to kill me for that little bit of shit. You can have it."

"Nigga, take yours like I take mines: like a muthafuckin G," Pound said, squeezing off three shots.

BOOM! BOOM! BOOM! The point blank range shots went into the goon's chest and exited out the back, knocking doorknob size holes out of him.

Pound and Taz trotted to the whip where Boot smashed out, leaving Johnny Boys parking lot a bloody mess.

*****

Diego flicked ashes out the window of his Lexus from the blunt of purp he was smoking on. He was frustrated as fuck. He was parked down from TaTa's house. He kept staring at the FOR SALE sign that was posted in the front yard. Diego had called the number on the sign three different occasions, trying to see if the realtor would disclose any info on how he could get in contact with Tata. Every single call ended with the same result: nada.

Diego even tried to pillow talk the whereabouts out of Ski, but she claimed that she hadn't seen Tata or heard from her since Rico's funeral. Diego was starting to think desperately. He was thinking about setting an appointment up with the realtor to see the house and once the realtor got there, he would make her give him Tata's info at gun point.

Diego figured if he could find Tata, he could find Phatmama. But snatching the realtor would be reckless, and another reckless move he couldn't afford right now. His Uncle Cain was all on his ass when he found out about his so-called homeboys getting smashed at the cemetery. Diego gave Cain some lame-ass excuse that his homie got smashed behind some mistaken identity shit and that he didn't know the identities of the people that murked his so-called friends. Little did Cain know Diego didn't even fuck with them niggas like that.

In his eyes, they were soft. But Cain was kind of happy about the incident. He always complained about Diego fucking with them young niggas anyway. Diego told his flunkies if they kidnapped Phatmama or killed her, Cain would put them on the payroll. But shit turned out so badly for them.

It was getting late. Diego started the Lex up. He was going to swing by Ski's mom's crib to check up on them. He had dropped Ski off over there a few hours ago. Ski and her mother weren't getting along. Their relationship had turned strange since Rico got murdered. Ski's mom was knocked up and she was ready to have the baby in the next few months.

Diego stopped by the liquor store and copped himself a bottle of Remy VSOP and a pack of Backwoods. From there, he hit KFC and grabbed two boxes of chicken with mashed potatoes, biscuits, and mac and cheese.

He knew that Ski and her mom would probably be hungry by the time he slid through there. The chicken was smelling good as a muthafucka. Diego couldn't wait to get the finger-licking chicken in his mouth.

Fifteen minutes later, Diego was pulling in the Silver Springs apartment complex where Ski's mom lived. He parked the Lexus in the front of the building, gathered the food, and made his way to Ski's mother's apartment. He tapped on the door with the black Foamposites on his feet. Diego looked fresh to death in his cream-colored Moss Brown sweat suit.

Tina, Ski's mom, opened the door, displaying her swollen belly. Despite the fact that she was pregnant, Tina was very attractive. Her Latin features were very strong.

"Hey Tina, I brought you and my baby something to eat," Diego said, holding the bags of KFC up in the air.

Tina rolled her eyes and stepped to the side to let Diego in. Diego didn't know what was wrong with Tina, but she used to be real pleasant with him, especially when she found out that Cain was his uncle. But now he could tell that she was really annoyed with him. He didn't know if it was due to the pregnancy or the fact she realized he was two years older than her daughter. But whatever it was, she needed to get her shit together because he was ready to check her on her bullshit.

Ski walked out from the back room and saw Diego walking in with some food and looking handsome as ever. She smiled hard and rushed to love on him. She wrapped her arms around his neck and planted kisses all over his face.

"Hey bae!" Ski said in between kisses. "I miss you so much." Ski buried her face in the crook of Diego's neck and inhaled the black coconut oil that he often scented his skin with.

"I miss you too, baby," Diego replied.

Meeting Ski had been good for Diego He couldn't fathom all the emotions that lived inside of him when it came to Ski. He had never felt what he felt when he was with Ski.

Tina sucked her teeth and took the bags away from Diego while her daughter still hugged him. Tina put the food on the kitchen table and went to her room without saying a word. Ski heard her mom suck her teeth and once Tina was out of their presence, she spoke on it.

"That bitch getting on my nerves. I tried to talk with her, but she would barely speak to me, and every time I ask her what she's going through, she just starts crying. I'm just frustrated with her right now," Ski explained to Diego. "I was gonna spend the night with her, but it's clear she needs to be by herself. I want to go to your crib, Diego," Ski stated.

"A'ight, we can do that, but first, let's eat and burn some of this bud while we catch a movie, then we can head to my place," Diego said, leading Ski to the kitchen where Tina had left the food on the table.

Ski pulled two plates from the cabinet from over top of the kitchen sink. She began to empty the KFC from its bags and placed the food on the plates. Once the plates were full and the table was set, Ski and Diego were ready to eat.

"Hold up, baby, go get yo' moms and ask her to join us," Diego suggested.

"Nawl, she ain't gonna want to eat with us and I don't feel like dealing with attitude," Ski complained.

"No, baby, go ask her anyway. She's pregnant and she needs to eat."

Ski rolled her eyes and stomped off to fulfill her man's request.

Tina sat in her dimly-lit bedroom with her door closed. Tears crept down her eyes. It'd been a month since Rico was murdered. Tina still hadn't begun to heal. She didn't even know how to heal. Hell, she didn't even know how she was going to manage without Rico. She know she was dead-ass wrong for fucking around with her sister Tata's man. But the heart loves who it loves. When Rico found out that she was pregnant, he was delighted and overwhelmed when he found out that she was having his first son. Rico had promised that he was going to leave Tata and grant Tina a family like she always desired.

Tina wiped her tears away, thinking about her lover. She rubbed her stomach, thinking about the day Rico brought her the cocaine-white QX 60 Infiniti truck. Tina and Rico were laid up at the W after one of their many sex session because they always found themselves getting it in. A commercial came on TV showcasing the truck. The next morning when they were leaving the hotel and waiting for valet parking to bring Rico's Benz around, instead of his 600 pulling up, the prettiest white Infiniti QX 60 stopped in front of them, sitting on some black 22 rims and sporting a big red bow on its hood. Tina looked confusedly at her lover. Rico tipped the valet worker.

"Rico, this not your truck," Tina said, realizing this was the same truck she told Rico that she liked.

"I know. It's yours," Rico stated, smiling and showing all his teeth.

Tina fell deeper in love with Rico.

Coming back from the past, Tina's hand trembled as she reached under the pillow and removed the 32 revolver that Rico had given to her for protection.

She couldn't live without her baby daddy. Tina had plans to take hers and the baby's life so they could spend forever in heaven with Rico. Tina placed the gun in her mouth with a shaky hands. She cocked the hammer back on the small gun.

Tina took a deep breath and with teary eyes she mumbled. "Please God, forgive me." Her damp finger touch the trigger in the trigger guard.

"Aye Ma!" Ski walked into her mother's room without knocking. "What the…? No, Ma, no!"

Ski rushed over to her mother's side. Tina snatched the gun out of her mouth and pointed it at her daughter.

"Get the fuck back!" Tina shouted, stopping Ski in her tracks. "Just get out. I just want to die and be with Rico, my child's father," Tina said, scooting back on her bed, still holding Ski at bay with the gun.

Suddenly Tina's statement made it clear to Ski what her mother was going through.

Diego appeared in the doorway after hearing all the commotion.

"No, Ma, you can't kill yourself and my baby brother. We got to get them back for killing Rico," Ski said, fishing her phone out of her back pocket. Her hands shook hard, fumbling with her phone as her fingers tapped on the screen of her phone. Ski hit play on her iPhone and what spilled out of Ski's phone just provoked Tina to a new level of hate for Tata. She finally had proof that Tata had committed the murder.

CHAPTER 9

"Man, I'm telling ya, slim, that bitch Tata is a treacherous, cold-hearted bitch," Diesel stated as he passed the Backwood to his cousin Bull.

"Come on, cuzzo, you putting a 10 on a 1. I just can't see that fine, sexy, chocolate muthafucka chopping a whole fuckin' body up. We talking about your man and a nigga that she shared the same bed with! Slim, you talking about this bitch like she got some type of super powers or some shit." Bull was getting annoyed by the weakness Diesel was displaying for this board. "We can't be talking about the same Tata that you was fucking behind your man's back?" Bull asked.

Diesel's body turned warm from embarrassment. "Yeah, I dib and dabbed in the pussy a few times, but a nigga wasn't sprung out and in love and shit," Diesel said, lying through his teeth. Diesel was mad that Tata cut ties with him after Rico's murder.

"Whatever, nigga, that shit ain't about nothing," Bull said, but he really knew that his cousin was soft for a big butt and a smile. "So what's the game plan when this bitch get here?" Bull questioned.

"Cuz, if this slimy-ass bitch doesn't have my paper, I'm pushing her shit back straight like that." Diesel was referring to the money that Tata had gotten for the jewels that she sold to Rau'f from the McCormick & Smit heist. Diesel was kinda leery to meet Tata like she requested. He still didn't know who put the Feds on Rico. It could have been his crime partner, Tone. Tone got in the wind after he mistakenly shot an off-duty FBI agent doing the McCormick & Smit robbery. But if he had to bet his life on it, Tata was behind Rico being wanted by the Feds and his death. It just seemed odd that Rico was killed soon after the Feds started looking for Rico in connection to the FBI agent being killed. Rico popped up dead that same night and Tata ended up with the jewels from the heist.

Diesel studied the parking lot for any sings of Tata. He checked his Rolex and it was 11:15 p.m. He had picked the place to meet Tata: behind McKinley Tech high school. The parking lot was dark and it was out of the way from sight.

"You think the bitch gonna show?" Bull asked as he lit a cigarette.

"Man, I hope so. I need my fuckin' money and I need this bitch dead."

Diesel's phone vibrated on his lap. He had a text from Tina and it read: DON'T TRUST THE BITCH TATA. CALL ME ASAP! Before Diesel could call Tina and find out what the fuck was going on, a set of headlights entered the parking lot. Diesel saw the midnight blue Infiniti G37 that Tata was pushing. He paused on calling Tina. Tata parked a few feet away. She got out of her truck and scanned the parking lot. Diesel watched her intently. Tata strutted her way towards Diesel. Despite the darkness, you still could tell that Tata was stacked from the dim light that was provided by the security light that was on the side of the school. "

"Damn, cuzzo, Tata's ass phat, shit! You sure you want to body the broad?" Bull asked for confirmation.

"Just hold fast, Bull. I just got a text from Tina saying don't trust this bitch. I want to find out what the fuck is going on because Tata and Tina is sisters, and if this bitch's own sister is talking about don't trust her, then I know some trifling shit is going on and I want to know about it."

Tata got closer and saw that Diesel was rolling with someone. She shook her head and climbed in the back seat of his Range Rover. "Wassup, Diesel?" Tata greeted him. Tata's demeanor was pissy so Diesel replied with a bullshit reply.

"That muthafuckin' check."

The vibe in the truck felt strange. Tata sensed danger, but she kept it Red Bottom Squad-like: calm and cool.

"I detect some hostility in this bitch." Tata let it be known that she felt the bad energy in the truck's cabin.

"It's not hostility. I just want what's mines and a few questions answered," Diesel stated through clenched teeth while staring at Tata though his rearview mirror.

Bull sat there slightly shaking his head at his cousin's weakness. Bull felt that Diesel should have secured the bag before he started doing all this damn talking.

"Psssss!" Tata let out a deep breath. She knew that Diesel was going to ask her about her pulling back from him. "What you want to know?" Tata blurted out.

"How you find someone to buy the jewels for you from the heist?"

"Look, Diesel, I'm not about to reveal my connects to you, and what difference does it make? I got your money for the jewels," Tata retorted, staring Diesel in his eyes back through the rearview mirror.

"Did you have something to do with Rico being killed?" Diesel asked, turning around in in the Range Rover seat to watch Tata's body language.

"What the fuck's up with you and all these weird-ass questions? Why the fuck you want to know?" Tata's voice rose a little.

Bull wasn't feeling how Tata was addressing his cousin. But he kept his mouth shut and gritted his teeth.

"Because I believe that you and them bitches that you be with offed my fucking man just so you could get your hands on them jewels."

"Your man! Was Rico your fucking man when you was eating my pussy or when you was serving me them back shots? If so, then you had a fucked-up way of showing that Rico was your man."

Bull chuckled at Tata's comment. From that comment, he started to like Tata's vibe.

Diesel couldn't really recover from Tata's comment, so he went for broke. "What happen to us? I thought that we was going to be together?"

"We was together, and that shit ran its course. Some people are together for a lifetime. Some people are together for a season, and others for a reason. Diesel, we was together for a reason," Tata said with venom in her voice. "Now do you want your money or not? Because I got shit to do."

Even though the truck AC was running, Diesel's body still became heated. Tata's words had his anger running hot. "Yeah, bitch, go get mines," Diesel replied with hate written all over his face.

"I'm not gonna comment on you calling me a bitch, but know this will be the last time you call me a bitch. I knew your ass was going to be bitter about the break up. But that's your problem, not mines. I'm going to give you Tone's cut of the money also, if you cool with that."

Diesel didn't say another word. He just looked at her crazy. He had made up his mind that once Tata gave him the money, he was fucking her up.

"The money is in my truck. I'm going to get it. I'ma be right back," Tata said, climbing out of Diesel's truck.

Diesel watched Tata as she walked to her truck. He started to think about the extra money that he was about to receive from Tone's cut from the heist.

"Man, you should let me jump out and pop this bitch with her slick-ass mouth," Bull stated, cutting into Diesel's thoughts.

"Nah, chill, nigga, I already told you what's good. But I'm fucking her ass up though, soon as she drops that bag in my hands."

Tata reached her truck and opened the back hatch and dug inside. Out of nowhere, sparks started sparking like a lighter. The windows in Diesel's truck dropped and the Range began to rock hard from taking on the impact of the assault rifle that Billie viciously finger fucked.

YAK-YAK-YAK-YAK-YAK-YAK-YAK!

Billie appeared from the shadow off the side of the school. Bull's chest and face opened up, spraying the truck interior with his blood. Tata came out the back of her truck with a chrome fo'-fifth equipped with an extended clip. She opened fire and advanced towards Diesel's whip.

Diesel got low in his seat and knocked the truck into gear and floored it. He had been put in a trick bag by Tata. He was determined to make it up out of this situation and pay her ass back.

More shots rained down on Diesel truck. A bullet hit Diesel in his thigh and another one slammed into his chest. His vision blurred instantly and as he was making way out of the high school parking lot, he crashed into a Dodge Durango.

His lights went out.

*****

Jelli was in her bag with Tata. She couldn't understand why she would bring Racks' dyke ass into the clique. She didn't even know Racks. The way that Tata was moving was going to get them all sent back to prison. And on top of all that bullshit, she was going to bring Billie's cracker ass on board after all that shit they had been through with them crackers in the mountains in Hazelton, WV.

Jelli know that she had to start falling back from the Red Bottom Squad. She didn't want to voice her opinion at the meeting because she had already decided she was going to pull two more jobs with the group and then she was out. She had plans to open up to Cain about her past and straight focus on their future together.

Jelli lay across the bed and Cain's handsome face appeared out of nowhere. She smiled and knew that Cain was her King. No man was fit for her other than Cain. All Jelli wanted from Cain was for him to love her. She had never experienced true love.

Jelli been on her own since the age of eleven. She came from a dysfunctional family. Her dad suffered from mental health issues and her mom just didn't give a fuck about her. She was often lonely, abused, and hungry. And when she went to do her bid in the feds, her brother and sister barely checked up on her. At this point, she didn't even know where her siblings were. All she had was Cain to love her.

Her mentally ill dad once told her, "Always follow your heart."

And Jelli had plans to do so.

CHAPTER 10

"Come on, Phatmama, you got to put that shit out. We riding around with a whole fucking brick of heroin and we got guns. You don't need to be burning the loud pack now," Tata said, cracking the window on Phatmama's truck so the strong scent of weed could escape the truck while fresh air rushed in.

"Since when you start being scared to ride dirty and smoke something?" Phatmama stated with an attitude, but she mashed the Backwood out in the truck's ashtray.

"I'm not scared, but we got to move better than what we been moving," Tata retorted.

"Yeah, whatever!" Phatmama said, checking her mirrors. "So how did my girl do last night?"

Tata smirked. "Very impressive. Billie handled her business."

Tata had taken Billie on a hit last night to body Diesel. She wanted to see for herself what the white chick was really made of first hand. Billie followed orders without hesitation. Billie had earned her spot on the Red Bottom Squad last night. "If Billie demonstrates those same traits on our next job that she executed last night, we going to come up real quick. Billie was 'fearless'!" Tata worked her hands in quotation marks.

Phatmama nodded her head up and down. She was proud of Billie.

"So what you think gonna happen at this meeting?" Phatmama asked, trying to get a better understanding of what Tata had in mind.

"I really don't know what to expect. All I'm shooting for is for Whip to hear me out for the most part. Then accept my offer and loan us Racks to pull off a few licks."

"I hope so, but let me ask this. If this shit works, then what?" Phatmama inquired.

"Then we get money money! We hit a few licks, rob Cain, and kill his ass. Open up a club or a luxurious and lucrative escort service, something that we can stack money and keep us out them white people's jewelry stores," Tata stated, laughing. "I appreciate you giving up the heroin so we can have a bargaining tool with Whip."

"Girl, no need to thank me. What I got belongs to the Red Bottom Squad. What was I gonna do with fifteen bricks of heroin?" Phatmama plugged the aux cord up to her phone to play some music. She had been feeling Rick Ross's new album *Port of Miami 2*. She found her favorite track on the album and hit play. The song "Running the Streets" came through her truck speakers and Phatmama began to rap along with the Miami native.

"Fake niggas always caught up in the realist shit. Mama always told me watch who you be dealing wit'. Snake niggas you can't get wrapped up in ur feelings wit'. Never watered down my bitches on some killing shit." Phatmama rocked back and forth in her seat. There was something about the song that placed her in a zone. She put the song on repeat and listened to the song three times before they pulled up around big 3-0 in front of Whip's trap house.

Tata pulled her phone out her and double-checked the address that Racks had text her. Tata sent Racks a quick text letting her know she was outside. Tata noticed Billie and Zoey pull up across the street from the trap. Tata wanted to have some back up just in case shit didn't go as plan.

A few fiends were littered around the trap house, but it was obvious that Whip and his people weren't making much at this spot. Tata knew that it was from the lack of product or even worse, the lack of hustle.

The door to the trap house opened and Racks stepped out and waved them in. Tata grabbed the bag that rested between her Red Bottoms and made her way inside the trap house. Phatmama walked behind her while scanning her surroundings.

When Tata and Phatmama walked into the house a light sour odor hit their nose and their eyes fell on a black tar baby-looking muthafucka with a piece of his bottom lip missing.

Whip sat on a red leather bean bag chair. Tata couldn't read his eyes through his bifocals that he wore. About five of his foot soldiers were posted throughout the room. Racks took a seat next to Whip on a red milk create.

"Hey Whip," Tata said, extending her hand to him.

"What's poppin'?" Whip replied and accepted her hand.

Something happened when their hands touched. His rough hand and Tata's soft hand felt right together, like it was a perfect match. Like peanut butter and jelly. Tata felt a strange energy that passed through their touch. It wasn't bad energy, but one that felt pleasant.

"I want to thank you for meeting with me and Phatmama."

"The only reason why I'm entertaining this meeting with you is because you generously donated them twenty bands to my organization. So with that being said, let's get this meeting started," Whip said.

Phatmama and the oil-black dude stared at one another.

"Well, I was anticipating a sit down with just you and Racks so we could try to come up with some type of agreement."

"Naw, we good, speak your piece," Whip retorted.

This wasn't going how Tata had planned. She had to think fast. Sometimes being bold is the best move a person could make. She dug in the bag that she was carrying and pulled out the brick of heroin and tossed it to Whip. He caught it in midair. Once it soaked in what he held in his hand, he sat up straight on the bean bag.

"Aye, clear this bitch! I want every muthafucka in here on post."

The men in the room moved fast. Racks and the grimy-looking dude remained in the room with Whip.

"Okay, Tata, you got my attention. Speak your business," Whip stated while flipping the brick over in his hand. He could smell the heroin through its package.

"I want to help build your nation."

"And how are you going to do that?" the oil can-black dude finally spoke.

Tata look at him and back at Whip for permission to keep speaking.

"That's my right hand right there. That's my nigga Boot," Whip said. Boot nodded his head towards Tata.

"We want to supply you. I want to be your plug. I can give you the work for cheap and in return, all we seeking is your protection."

"What the fuck type of shit you bitches into?" Boot blurted out.

"Hold the fuck up! I'm not your bitch. And we into getting this muthafuckin' bag. Just because we have a pussy between our legs doesn't mean we are not capable of holding our own, because we can get this shit cracking just like any other nigga out here in these streets." Phatmama was heated at how Boot was trying to handle them.

Boot jumped to his feet, but before he could react, Whip waved him off.

"Chill, Blood. Treat the ladies with some respect," Whip stated. He didn't want to blow this deal. He knew that the dope was high grade because the smell that was reeking through the package was potent. "Tata, break the situation down so I can get a better understanding," Whip suggested.

Tata broke everything down, but left out the details that Phatmama murdered for the dough and one of the bricks he held in his hand was a result of her being what Destiny Skai called in her book *A Fetti Girl*.

"So how do Racks come to play in all of this?" Whip wanted to know.

"We got a few licks that we need help to pull and we would like to bring Racks in on the licks." Tata replied.

"What type of caper are you talking about?" Boot questioned.

"That's not open for discussion. The licks that we pull are too lucrative and high risk to disclose any info about them," Phatmama interjected and stated firmly.

Whip flipped the brick over in his hand and saw the Red Canadian leaf stamped on the package.

"What's the ticket on the brick?" Whip asked.

"That one right there is for free. I did my homework and I know that a brick is running for 100 bands to 125 bands in this city. But I'll be charging you 75 bands a brick. So if you can accept our offer, then you are already paid with the brick and the 20 bands I sent you through Racks."

Whip sat the brick on the table in front of him and really took in Tata and Phatmama. They were offering him a deal of a life time. *How much protection these boss bitches need?* Whip thought to himself. He already knew that this brick in his hand was going to bring a lot of bread, and it was going to be coming in fast. He look over towards Boot and his partner gave him a slight nod of approval. "Racks, I'm going to let you rock with Tata and them for a minute."

"Red Bottom Squad," Tata corrected Whip.

"The Red Bottom Squad," Whip corrected himself. "But know that you are D.C.B. and I can pull your ass at any time."

Racks nodded in agreement.

A smile crept across Tata's pretty face. Tata walked over and shook Whip hand for the second time, and she was greeted with that same energy she felt earlier. Tata really paid attention to Whip and his shea butter-brown skin. His white, form-fitting Polo T-shirt showed off his broad shoulders and firm chest, which Tata admired. Him having a flat stomach enhanced his appearance. Whip stood 6 foot even. He was handsome, but what threw Tata the fuck off about him was the bifocals that he rocked like they were Versace frames. The lenses in Whip's glasses looked like ice cubes.

Tata had to shake her stare off Whip. She then went to give Boot a handshake. But instead of shaking her hand, he gave her a fist bump.

"Aye, I'm about to run. I got shit to do and a bag to secure. I got your digits on speed dial, Whip. I hope once I call, you don't hesitate to come guns blazing."

"One thing you going to learn about me and D.C.B.'s: we stand on honor. So don't worry about me honoring my word. I just hope that you can do the same."

"I wouldn't put the Red Bottom Squad name on it if I couldn't," Tata stated. "Racks, I'll hit you in a few days for a meeting."

Racks nodded her head. Tata passed her Chloe shades over her eyes and stepped out of the trap house feeling powerful.

"Blood, them hoes thicker than a Snickers, especially that redbone. I'm telling you now, I'm gonna make her my bitch," Boot said excitedly.

"Slow down, nigga, let's get this money. I want to play our hand right and see where this shit gonna lead us. Tata and them got more dope than we need and want, and if we gotta body a few niggas along the way, then fuck it. Tata just dropped us a whole fucking brick in our hands for free, so by all means, let's get this paper and build our Nation. Call an emergency meeting. I want the whole team at the dope table ready to cut and bag this shit up."

Jibril Williams

fiends littered the buildings in Wellington Park. Jelli looked at Cain when he stopped the Bentley in front of a building.

"I'm getting ready to show you all of me," Cain said, getting out of the Bentayga and leaving it running.

Jelli hesitated to get out, but she did once Cain beckoned her to. She got out and Cain draped an arm around her neck. Two young niggas stepped out of the crowd with PS9 Rugers that held thirty round extended clips. They escorted Cain and Jelli inside the building to the third floor. Outside a door, there was another one of Cain's goons. He nodded at the two escorts and they turned on their heels and went back the way that they came.

"You know that you left the car running, right?" Jelli stated.

"Yeah, babe, don't worry about that. It's in good hands," Cain replied.

The goon standing and guarding apartment 312 opened the door and let Cain and Jelli in. What Jelli saw reminded her of the scene in the movie *New Jack City*, where Nino Brown had a bunch of butt naked-ass women in the room packing up coke in small bottles. The only thing different with this scene was the naked women were placing a powdery substance in wax covered paper. Jell thought she had only read about or seen shit like this in movies.

A short, pretty, brown-skinned chick walked up and handed Cain and Jelli face masks the kind that the doctors use in the hospital.

"Wassup, Cat?" Cain greeted the woman.

Jelli watched one of the naked workers place a blue stamp on the wax paper after she filled it with heroin.

"You know, just running this ghetto sweat shop like it's a Fortune 500 club."

"I see that!" Cain replied. He grabbed Jelli's hand and led her down the hall to a room on the right. The room was filled with another five naked women and a goon sitting in a corner chair watching them like a staring pit bull. The women were counting the stamped packages

"Dez, is everything good in here?" Cain asked as he broke through the threshold of the door.

"Yeah, boss, everything is running like clockwork in here," Dez replied.

The women in the room didn't even look up from their counting. Jelli wondered why Cain was showing her all of this. Cain then led her out of the apartment.

"Why you showing me all of this, Cain?" Jelli inquired.

Cain stopped and faced her. "I want you to know how I make my money. I don't want to keep no more secrets from you."

Jelli studied Cain's face. There wasn't anything but seriousness in his features. Cain's eyes confirmed that he was sharing the same feelings that Jelli was having for him. She kissed his lips and Cain welcomed Jelli's lips. They shared a kiss for a few minutes that seemed like it lasted forever.

"I still have a bunch other shit to show you," Cain said, pulling away from Jelli's soft lips.

Jelli nodded her head up and down in agreement.

Once Cain and Jelli made it back outside, the Bentayga was still in its same spot, still idling with the doors open. "See? I told you it was in good hands," Cain said to Jelli, making a small joke of the concerns she had earlier.

Next Cain took Jelli to every trap house and business establishment he had in D. C. He broke down the ins and outs of his operation to her in fine detail. Jelli took everything in. She was astonished that Cain was on the level he was in the game. She kinda figured that he was selling drugs, but not on this level he just showed her.

She was wrestling with her thoughts as Cain drove the Bentley back to the house. She was wondering if it was a good time to confess to Cain how she got her money. Her heart was screaming, "Confess, bitch!", but her brain was like, "Don't be a dumb bitch. Pull two more licks, then confess to him." Jelli didn't want to confess and have Cain not be understanding about her profession. If Cain spazzed on her about her confession, then at least she would have a large enough bag to still break away from the Red Bottom Squad.

Cain was watching Jelli from the corner of his eye. He wasn't sure how she was digesting what she had seen and what he had conveyed to her today. But all he knew was he wanted Jelli to be his wife. He knew that he had broken a major rule today by showing his hand to

Jelli, but he didn't give a fuck. He was going to retire from his line of business in the next few months and sell the city to the Canadian Mob.

"Hey sexy," Cain said, placing his hand on Jelli's leg.

"What's up, baby?"

"I'm having a get together at Bass & Cru. Why don't you invite your friends? It's about time I meet them."

"I thought you said you didn't like meeting new faces," Jelli said, looking at her lover strangely.

"Well, times are changing. Let's get together and mingle," Cain suggested, showing off his pearly whites.

Jelli thought about it and thought it would be a good idea to finally introduce her girls to her man. Maybe they would understand when the time came as to why she wanted out the stick up game.

"Okay, I can make that happen. When is the get together?"

"In two weeks," Cain replied.

"Okay, then my girls will be there," Jelli said, smiling as she opened her legs and placed Cain's hand there.

Jibril Williams

CHAPTER 12

Diesel was propped up in his bed with tired eyes. He had been like this since he had made it home from the hospital. Diesel was furious that Tata tried to kill him. She managed to kill his cousin Bull, and the thought of this only made Diesel's anger intensify a hundred times over.

Diesel brought his hand up to his chest wound and it felt hot. He didn't know who was working with Tata, but he could rest assured that it was one of them shiesty-ass bitches that she was running around robbing shit with. He couldn't believe how fucking stupid he was to even fall for a bitch like Tata. When the shots banged out and he tried to escape, he could see Tata raising her gun and sending hot copper his way. A bullet had hit him in the chest, which caused him to black out. A day later he had woken up in the hospital. The nurse told him that he was shot and had crashed his Range into a parked car. That was a week ago.

The police came to visit Diesel in the hospital. They questioned him about the shooting and the murder of his cousin. Diesel refused to give 12 any info about the shooting. He had plans to issue out his own street justice to Tata. She was living by the gun, so she was definitely dying by it. The police didn't leave until they applied some pressure to Diesel though. They were threatening to charge him with the gun that his cousin had in his possession when he got killed. They were talking about possession of a firearm was nine-tenths of the law. Diesel had to hit his lawyer up and explain the situation to him. The lawyer informed him that until the police actually charged him with something, then it was just a scare tactic.

The pain in Diesel's chest started to become unbearable. He reached over and grabbed the bottle of Percocet that the doctors prescribed for him. He popped two 30mg and chased it down with some water. He wished that he had Tina's number so he could call her and find out what was going on with Tata. He couldn't call Tina because his phone had broken in the crash the night he got shot. But as soon as he was on his feet, Tina was the first person that he was going to pay a visit to.

*****

Tina rocked back and forth on her sectional sofa, rubbing her stomach and listening to the recording that Ski had recorded on her phone. Rico must've butt dialed Ski by accident.

Ski had caught the final minutes of Rico's life on her phone. Tina wiped the tears that leaked from her eyes. Tata didn't have to kill her unborn child's father. So what that he was her sister's man? She had a child growing inside of her, and Tata had no right to take that away from her child. Her child needed his father, despite the betrayal. Tina must have listened to the recording over fifty times. She had been waiting on Diesel to get in touch with her. She had sent him over a dozen texts and he failed to reply. So she had to put her plan together without him. She didn't really trust Diego, her daughter's boyfriend, because he was young. But she had no choice. Since she found out that Cain was his uncle and Diego told her about how Phatmama was responsible for the death of his cousin Rocco, she was more prone to include him in on her plan. Tina still hadn't confronted her daughter about her sleeping with Rico. She was going to hold that until she was good and ready.

CHAPTER 13

"Gotdamn, nigga! Them bitches dropped a torch in our hands with this work," Boot exclaimed.

It'd only been about week since Tata gave them the brick of heroin and the drug traffic had been jumping non-stop. Whip took the dope from Tata and went straight to the table and cut it with Fentanyl and bagged the dope up from $5 bags to $50 packs.

"Them divas got their hands on a sure enough thing," Whip stated as he counted a handful of greenbacks. The small table was filled with money that had not yet been counted.

The day before Whip came out with the work, he had members of D.C.B. pass out 1000 free samples of the dope and inform the dope fiends where they could cop the new product at. They say the best promotion is by word of mouth, and the news of the new dope had spread like a California wildfire.

"Bruh, the way this shit is moving, we gonna need to open a new spot," Boot stated, adding another $1,000 stack to the floor next to where he sat.

"I agree with you, Boot, but we don't want to rush nothing. What I'm focusing on is stacking this muthafucking paper so we can go back and cop another brick from Tata. We are like fifteen bands away from having that seventy-five bands for our next brick."

"I'm feeling, that but I think we can get that bag up quicker if we send a few Bloods out to Johnny Boys and open up shop."

"Johnny Boys?" Whip said with a frown on his face. "You talking about the same Johnny Boys where you left three muthafuckas dead?"

"Yup!" Boot said like he didn't have a care in the world.

Whip shook his head. He didn't like the idea. He didn't know what the fuck was wrong with Boot. He always wanted to do some of the wildest shit ever. "Naw, slim, shit too risky."

"Man, fuck that! It's our time to come up. We got a strong product and we got a crazy-ass team of young niggas that are ready to put in work for our set. So let's put our stamp down. I been peeping shit out at Johnny Boys. You got a few young stragglers out there with some garbage-ass dope. We can pull up on them fools give them an option to join us and get some real money or die."

Whip was thinking about what his childhood friend was saying and he was right. They needed the spot, and it was time they put their stamp down. "A'ight, I want a six man team out there at Johnny Boys. Don't put no fucking hardhead-ass niggas out there. Put someone that we can count on. I want you to oversee them from the shadows. I don't want your face out there unless you have to."

Hearing this, Boot got excited on the inside. He knew that he was about to take D.C.B.'s to the next level with the Johnny Boys move. "Big homie, you a good nigga too. I just wanted to tell you that," Boot said.

"Come on, Boot, with all that mushy-ass shit. But why you say that though?" Whip questioned his friend.

"Because when Racks delivered them twenty bands from Tata, you didn't pocket nay fucking dollar. You gave every member of our organization a grand each," Boot stated. He placed another stack of money next to the first stack on the floor. "Why did you do that?" Boot asked.

Whip continued to count the money in his hand. He looked up from this count. "Loyalty is priceless, Boot. That's why I broke bread with them. When I eat, we all eat. That's the position of a boss." Whip just dropped a street jewel on Boot. "You take care of your people and they will take care of you."

Boot knew that Whip just spoke a mouthful, but he had crazy trust issues and he wasn't going to speak on them.

"I'm feeling that, bruh," Boot said.

The light tap at the door stopped Whip and Boot's money counting. Boot got out of the wooden chair and snatched his fo'-fifth off his hip and went to answer the door. No one knew where he lived except Whip and Racks, but he still was cautious. He looked out the peephole without saying "who is it?" On the other side of the door was Racks. He opened the door and shook it up with their gang handshake.

"What up though?" Racks greeted him.

"D.C.B.'s all day every day," Boot shot back at Racks. Boot closed the door behind his young homie and followed her to the front room, where Whip was still counting money.

"Swoop!" Racks yelled out, throwing up her B's on her hands, acknowledging her big homie.

"What's good, Racks?" Whip smiled.

"Just trying to make it happen on my end," Racks said, sliding the book bag off her shoulder. "Here goes the work for the trap."

Even though Whip allowed Racks to fuck with Tata and her squad, she still had a job to handle with her own peoples, and that was to pick up the pack from the stash house and make sure all the traps stayed fill with work.

"Just set it on the floor. I'll drop it off to Ink."

"I see ever since you taught that boy a hard lesson, he been on his B's like a muthafucka," Racks said, sitting down in a chair.

"Sometimes a hard lesson is the best lesson," Whip said nonchalantly. "But what's poppin' with Tata and them?" Whip asked.

"I really don't know for sure, but I'm about to head her way. We got a meeting. She want to go over the details of the lick she got for us."

"Is she really the plug, or she got a nigga that's filtering the work through her?" Boot chimed in, asking his own question.

"From what I've seen, Tata don't have a man." This made Whip tune in on what Racks was saying. "Every time I been in her presence, it's been her and the clique," Racks said, smiling and eyeing the stack of money on the floor and table.

"Listen, Racks, I want you to learn everything you can about Tata and her crew. I know it's something that she ain't telling us, but that goes with the game," Whip stated.

"A'ight, I'm on it, but let me get going. I don't want to be late." Racks shook it up with her two homies and headed to the door.

"Oh, Racks, tell that thick redbone muthafucka Phatmama I said get at a nigga and I like 'em thick."

Racks just shook her head at Boots's comment as she headed out the door.

*****

The inconspicuous blue Kia eased into a parking space two

buildings away from Diesel's apartment. The car's occupant studied his surroundings, looking for anything that seemed out of the ordinary. He laid his head back on the head rest and lit a cigarette. A couple of months ago he wouldn't dare indulge in smoking a cancer stick, but the drastic changes in his life had him smoking a pack a day. A mangy cat slowly strolled across the parking and found a home under a white Honda.

The driver checked the cylinder of his Bulldog 44, satisfied that the Rhino slugs in the gun were ready to do some damage if need be. He was ready to go. He slapped the cylinder closed and flicked the butt of the Newport out the window. He stepped out of the Kia, stored the 44 on his hip, and pulled his black T-shirt over the handle of the gun. He made his way to see the nigga Diesel.

He let his knuckles tap on the door. He waited in silence, trying this best to hear some movement on the other side of the door. He look around and checked the time on his Oyster Master Rolex. The watch was all he had to his name. It was only months ago he had to flee D.C. with 110 bands. Thirty thousand of that money came from Diesel as a loan and the other eighty came from a last minute caper he had pulled on a set of twins. He fled to Miami because a jewelry store robbery went wrong and he shot an off-duty FBI agent. So he went down South to start over. But living in Miami, the price of living was high and the beautiful women there were even more expensive than the cost of living. The money that he went to Miami with was easily depleted. Now he was back in D.C. lurking. His knuckles rapped across the door again. He was thinking about sliding back through a little later until he heard a voice on the other side of the door.

"Who the fuck is it?" Diesel said, snatching the door open and staring into the face of an old friend.

"What's up, slim? I heard them crackas murked Rico," Tone said, holding his arms open.

Diesel stepped into Tone's embrace. Diesel winced in pain from his healing gunshot wounds.

"Naw, slim, it wasn't them crackas. It was them vicious-ass bitches that Rico had up under him."

The statement Diesel made had Tone wondering. The men broke

their embrace.

"D, what the fuck you talking about? The word I hear is that the Feds got on Rico's line and when they went to arrest him, they killed him," Tone said.

"Man, come in and let me break the change of events down to you. Shit crazy as a muthafucka," Diesel said as he escorted Tone into his apartment. Diesel locked the door behind them.

It had been a minute since Tone had been in Diesel's apartment, but things still looked the same. The navy blue leather sofa sat in front of an oak coffee table with matching end tables that sat on each end of the sofa. You could tell that Diesel was going through something because he was somewhat of an OCD type of nigga and the way that the clothes and carry out containers littered the living room of his apartment told a tale that Diesel was off his square.

Diesel knocked some clothes that were decorating the sofa to the side and eased himself down on the sofa. Tone took a seat on a bar stool. He could see that Diesel was in distress. It was all over his face.

"Tone, I'm jive glad that you showed up when you did. That bitch is a dick-eating snake. That bitch killed my cousin, shot me, and left me for dead."

"Cut the bullshit, Diesel. Tata killed your cousin and popped you too?" Tone said with a little bit of excitement in his voice.

"Yeah, bruh. When you left the city, the Feds came swooping in looking for Rico for the FBI murder," Diesel said, unscrewing the top off a half-drunk bottle of Bacardi 501 that he swiped from the coffee table in front of him.

The mention of the murdered agent broke Tone out in hives. He watched Diesel take a big gulp from the bottle.

"I think Tata tipped 12 about the robbery and the agent's murder," Diesel said, taking another swig from the bottle. Diesel continued, "The Feds just missed Rico. He went into hiding, and the only person that knew where he was located was Tata. The night he was murdered, he called me and told me that he sent Tata to grab his stash and to take the merchandise from the heist to his people to exchange for cash. He told me once Tata came back with Zoey from getting the money, he was going to put a bullet in them bitches because they knew too much.

I guess them bitches was one step ahead of Rico because Rico ended up dead. They chopped his body up, Tone," Diesel said, staring off into nothing like he was playing the event out in in his head.

The new info that Diesel conveyed to Tone left his mind boggled. This was no way that those four sexy-ass bitches could have the nerves to chop a whole human being up. He was just not buying it. They must have had some male accomplice with them.

"You know them bitches living big on that money from the McCormick & Smit heist," Diesel stated, looking at Tone.

"You know that I came to get my cut of that money. I don't really know what the fuck you and them bitches got going on, but all I want is my fucking money," Tone confessed.

Diesel balled his face up. "What you mean you just want your money? I just told you that them hoes chopped Rico's body up."

"Man, fuck Rico. Whatever the bitches done to him, he deserved it," Tone said, revealing how he truly felt about Rico. "Remember how that nigga played me after that heist went wrong?" Tone spoke with pure anger in his voice.

Diesel immediately reflected back to that day and a light switch was turned on in his head. It wasn't Tata that put 12 on Rico. It was this bitch-ass nigga that was sitting in front of him.

"You bitch-ass nigga! It was you that that put the Feds on Rico. You rat bitch!" Diesel screamed.

"You damn right I did. I mailed in some jewelry that had Rico's fingerprints on it," Tone said as he upped his 44 on Diesel. Diesel swallowed the set of words that he had on the tip of his tongue upon seeing the big-ass gun Tone pulled out. "Bitch-ass nigga, don't move." Tone rose to his feet, clutching the gun firmly in his right hand. Tone walked over to Diesel and searched his waistline for a burner and came up empty.

"Tone, what the fuck you doing, nigga?" Diesel stuttered. His mouth instantly became dry.

"Nigga, shut all that soft-ass shit up and take me to the fucking safe," Tone said so aggressively that spit sprinkled from his mouth. Tone knew that Diesel didn't really care too much for him, so he wasn't about to show the nigga no mercy.

Diesel slowly made his way up off the sofa. He was moving too slowly for Tone's liking, so he assisted Diesel by snatching him by his shirt. Diesel's body crashed to the floor. The impact aggravated Diesel's raw bullet wounds. His chest and shoulder were inflamed with pain.

"Get your punk ass up!" Tone yelled, standing over Diesel.

Diesel breathed heavily through his nose. The fresh pain he was experiencing had him light headed. He struggled to his feet. "I'm gonna take you to the safe, but please, slim, don't kill me. This shit ain't about nothing," Diesel pleaded with a raspy voice.

"The more your bitch ass wastes time talking, your hoe ass is closer to seeing God."

Diesel led Tone to his safe without saying another word. His mind was racing along with his heart. He weighed the chances of him getting to his extra gun in his safe. Out of all places, he had left his 9mm on the night stand next to his bed. If he was lucky enough to get the gun from the safe, would he be fast enough to up it on Tone and kill his ass? His bullet wounds had his confidence shot. Diesel spun the dial on the safe that was located in his spare bedroom. Tone kept the 44 pressed against the back of Diesel head. With every spin of the dial, Tone ground his gun into Diesel's skull, breaking his skin.

The eighty-five pound safe popped open and before Diesel could fully open the safe door, Tone yanked him by his shirt and flung him to the floor.

"I got it, nigga," Tone said, walking over to the bed and removing a pillow case from a pillow. Tone started loading Diesel's money and jewels into the pillow case. When Tone saw the high point Brownie 380 sitting in the safe, he became angry. If he would have slipped and let Diesel empty the safe for him, Diesel definitely would have gone for the gun.

Diesel laid on the floor. He stared at Tone then back at the 12 gauge that laid on the floor under the bed. Diesel knew that it was now or never. Tone took his eyes off Diesel to go back in to safe for the remainder of the money and Diesel made his move. He scrambled hard on the floor like an NFL football player that pushed hard through a defensive line to gain the one yard for a touchdown. Diesel's hand touched the stock of the 12 gauge and things went into slow motion for him.

Things happened so fast for Tone that by the time he realized what was happening by looking over his shoulder, he saw Diesel pulling a mean-looking shotgun from under the bed. Tone's survival instincts kicked in and his cannon exploded in his hand.

BOOM-BOOM-BOOM! A 44 slug tore through Diesel's lower back and another ripped through the center of his back while the third slug went wild. Diesel's body began to spasm. He laid face down with his hand still resting on the butt of the shotgun. The rise and fall of his back inform Tone that he was still alive.

Tone walked over to Diesel and pushed him on his back with the foot of his Nike boot. Diesel stared up at Tone, blood spilling from his mouth. He never thought that it would be Tone who took him out. Diesel fought hard to breathe. The lower part of his back felt cold and the feeling of numbness trickled down to his legs. Diesel choked on his own blood as it filled his lungs. Still holding eye contact with Tone, he used his last bit of strength to muster up his final words.

"You rat bitch!"

BOOM! Tone's 44 sounded off one last time, knocking the contents of Diesel's head onto the floor. Tone walked out of Diesel's apartment seventy bands richer and with a couple of piece of jewelry. Now he was on a mission to locate Tata to get what she owed him.

CHAPTER 14

"We gonna hit Bank of America on South Capital," Tata stated, watching the faces of her team.

Racks gave Tata a strange look, but she didn't say shit at the moment. She figured Tata was a thorough type of bitch. She didn't think she was the type to go up in them white folks' bank and take their money. The Red Bottom Squad was on some *Set It Off* type of shit, Racks thought to herself with a smirk on her face.

"We hitting the bank on the busiest day of the month, which is four days from now," Tata spoke confidently, rubbing her hands together. She had become comfortable leading the team.

"Why the Bank of America? Why we diverting away from the jewelry stores?" Jelli asked with concern in her voice. All Jelli could do was think about how she spent seven years in the Feds for driving a getaway car on a bank heist.

"We just trying to keep the Feds off our ass. We want to keep them guessing our next move. We don't want to be predictable and plus dealing with the banks, we get cash instead of jewels. The way that I figure, why double hustle? Why hit a jewelry store then turn around and have to sell the merch for cash when we can just grab the cash and keep it moving?" Tata stated.

Jelli was Tata's girl, but she started to worry Tata in a way that made Tata not want to fuck with her. Jelli started to seem like the weakest link in the group.

"We gonna to hit the bank at 9 a.m. From my bank intel, the back vault will be open and the cash cow will be behind the middle bank teller. Zoey and Racks on the floor. You all job is to lay everyone face down and confiscate all phones," Tata instructed. "Jelli and me will take the tellers and hit the cash cow. But that's not our target. We are snatching the $400,000 that the Bank of America armored truck is picking up from the bank. Billie will be driving the getaway car and Phatmama will be on stand by for plan B if things go wrong."

Each woman was mentally sketching out their roles that had to take place for the robbery to be successful.

*****

Tone pulled up in the underground parking at the Woodner building on 16th Street NW. He exited his car, removing the blue Polo pillowcase off the passenger seat. He canvassed the parking garage. Feeling comfortable that his surroundings were safe, he made his way to the elevator. The Woodner building was one of those best-kept secrets in Northwest Washington D.C. The building was a twelve floor high rise that came equipped with a small mini market, barber shop, and massage parlor on the inside of the residence. The roof held a small bar and pool. The attendants of the building were of mixed race and they were of high working class - judges, corporate lawyers, CEO's, and private bankers - so it puzzled Tone how Cee-Cee was living amongst the elite and affording to live in the Woodner building. From his understanding, you had to go through a vetting process to be eligible to take residence in the high rise. Not only that, it was rumored that the rent was $4,300 and up, depending on the size of the apartment you were renting and the location of it.

The elevator stopped on the 9th floor. Tone stepped off, adjusted his cannon on his hip, and threw the Polo pillowcase over his left shoulder. Tone found apartment 904A with ease. He gave the thick cherry wood door a knock. Moments later, the door was opened and a sexy Cee-Cee rushed Tone.

"Baby!" Cee-Cee screamed, jumping into Tone's arms and throwing her legs around his waist. She seductively started planting kisses all over his face and neck.

Instantly, Tone could feel the vibrant heat that was jumping from between Cee-Cee's thighs. She had her coochie planted on Tone's stomach.

Tone kissed Cee-Cee and enjoyed the warmth of her tongue. He dropped the pillowcase on the floor and kicked the door closed with

82

his foot. Tone firmly grabbed Cee-Cee's backside and stuck his tongue deep into her throat, which she gladly and hungrily accepted. It had been a minute since they'd seen each other, and they were dying to fuck. Their sex was always intense.

Cee-Cee unwound herself from around Tone. She immediately wiggled out of the black leggings she wore and pulled her Fendi shirt over her head, exposing her perfect rounded melons. Cee-Cee stood in front of Tone wide-legged. Tone's eyes roamed Cee-Cee's body, taking in her sexiness. He found her body a work of God, all the way down to the light stretch marks that tatted her hips. Tone's eyes fell on Cee-Cee's slightly shaved glistening pussy lips. His mouth watered. He had to taste her nectar. Tone removed his gun and placed it in the pillowcase that rested next to his foot. He then removed his clothes in record speed.

Tone took a few more moments to admire Cee-Cee's body while he stroked himself to a hardness. Walking over to Cee-Cee, he kissed her again before he dropped to his knees, getting eye level with the pussy. The scent of Cee-Cee's love box was intoxicating. Tone pressed his nose into her mound and inhaled deeply. Tone draped one of Cee-Cee's thick legs over his shoulders and went to assaulting her pussy with long dog licks, causing her orgasm to build up quickly.

Cee Cee had the back of his head palmed like a basketball, pulling him deeper into her coochie. Having her pussy eaten in such a skillful manner just sent her into a frenzy. "Oh, Tone!" she cried.

This seemed to motivate Tone as he went ham on Cee-Cee's clit. She gripped the back of Tone's head firmer, holding him in place between her legs.

"I'm cumming! Oh shit, I'm cumming!" Cee-Cee yelled out as her body began to tremble and she squirted milky juices into Tone's mouth.

Tone lapped up her juices like he was a tomcat. Tone rose to his feet, letting Cee-Cee's leg fall from his shoulder. He spun Cee-Cee around and planted her breasts against the wall so that her chunky round ass was pressed up against his manhood. He gave that ass a slap and watched the wave ride on that round muthafucka.

"Oh baby, stop playing and get into this pussy."

Tone worked the head up and down Cee-Cee's slit, getting it lubricated like he wanted it. Finding her opening, he pushed deep into her all the way to the base of him. He held himself there, enjoying Cee-Cee's warmness that held him captive. Tone wanted to moan out her name so bad, but he didn't. He just took the sensation of Cee-Cee's pussy in. He could never get enough of her.

Tone and Cee-Cee had a strange relationship. He loved the woman's dirty drawers but for the life of him, he could never find it in him to trust Cee-Cee, despite the fact that she did all the shady shit in the world for him. He could not bond with her on that level. It was Tone who had put Cee-Cee on Rico's line. Rico thought it was by fate that he had met Cee-Cee, but it was Tone who orchestrated it all. The plan was for Cee-Cee to get close enough to Rico to find out where he was holding his cash at, but Cee-Cee's silly ass ended up getting pregnant with Rico's daughter Nikky. Tone and Cee-Cee stopped seeing each other because she told Tone she wasn't going to abort her pregnancy. Tone took that deed as an act of treason. He cut ties with Cee-Cee. The act forced Cee-Cee to seek Rico's aid with her daughter after she had the baby. Cee-Cee even entertained the thought of her and Rico being a family, but like most niggas running the streets, shit was all good in the beginning until the baby got there. Then they start ducking the responsibility that comes with being a father.

Tone started stroking in and out of Cee-Cee's wet hole feverishly. Her soft backside slapped up against Tone's pelvis hard and the contact sounded off. Cee-Cee arched her back, willing Tone to go deeper and harder. Tone was amazed at how good Cee-Cee's sex was after all this time they had been sexing one another over the years. Tone wore a mean fuck face as he served Cee-Cee his thick rod. He pumped harder into Cee-Cee.

"Oh, baby. You're so fucking deep in me. Fuck me, Tone. Fuck me please," Cee-Cee commanded.

Tone could feel his nut build up. Tone pumped furiously. The clapping of their bodies reverberated throughout the small hallway. If anyone walked past 904A, they could surely hear the two getting their fuck on the other side of the door.

"Ah! Fuck! I'm cumming," Tone grunted as he felt the cum about to erupt from the head of his dick.

"Cum for me, baby. Cum for Cee-Cee."

Tone pulled his love stick out of Cee-Cee's piping hot coochie and skeeted his load on her butt cheeks and in the crack of her ass.

"That's right, cum for me," Cee-Cee coaxed and watched Tone coat her booty with his nut.

Tone staggered to the living room with weak legs. Cee-Cee made a dash to the bathroom before the nut could drip off her ass and sour the carpet on the hallway floor. Tone sat on the couch wide-legged with his head laid back on the cushion. Cee-Cee came back with a wet washcloth and cleaned Tone's member.

Tone watched Cee-Cee with a lustful eye. He couldn't understand why he couldn't shake the scandalous-ass broad. They both knew they were bad for each other. Dangerous, like a moth drawn to a flame. Tone watch Cee-Cee's chunky heart-shaped ass shake with every move as she walked back to the bathroom to discard the wash cloth.

Tone looked around the spacious apartment. The black leather L-shaped couch sat pretty on the dark burgundy carpet. The glass coffee table with black and gold trimmings was clean and neat and held an ashtray with a copy of Destiny Skai's latest novel on it, *Corrupted by a Gangster 4*. As long as Tone could remember, Cee-Cee was a diehard fan of Lock Down Publications and Destiny was her favorite author. Off to the right, the apartment held a small kitchen. Cee-Cee came back into the room with hers and Tone's clothes in her hand. She tossed Tone his belongings, stepped back into her leggings, and replaced the Fendi blouse back over her 38's. Tone put his jeans back on and opted not to put his shirt back on.

"You want something to drink or eat, baby?" Cee-Cee asked, tying her micro braids into a thick ponytail.

"I'm good for now, baby. Let a nigga catch his breath," Tone said, still a little winded from their fuck session.

"Let me find out that you can't keep up with me no more," Cee-

Cee teased.

"Whatever!" Tone said with a smirk. "I see that you living good."

"Yup! It's nice, ain't it?"

"This shit flyer then a muthafucka. How you afford it?" Tone asked.

"Damn, you haven't been here a good thirty minutes and you trying to find out do a bitch got a bag or not," Cee-Cee pouted.

"Shit ain't even like that. I'm just asking questions. Why the fuck you so secretive? I hope that you don't have me laying up in another nigga's shit," Tone stated, trying to create a smoke screen from Cee-Cee putting his ass on blast.

Cee-Cee had been dealing with and loving Tone's ass long enough to know the man she was sitting next to was on some bullshit. "Asking a question is 'how you doing today, Cee-Cee? How is your daughter doing, Cee-Cee?' Them are questions. Not asking about how a bitch affords her shit. And for the record, I make good money at the bank."

"Yeah, but not enough to live in a building that collects and washes your weekly laundry, a building that has a mini market, barbershop, and a rooftop pool," Tone retorted, looking in Cee-Cee's eyes for the lie.

"Tata be breaking me off like every other week with money for me and Nikky."

Tone sat up straight on the couch. "You talking about Rico's Tata?"

"Yes, that's the Tata I'm talking about. I told you about that night she found me sitting on her and Rico's porch and I told her that Rico was Nikky's dad. She told me that she was Nikky's father from now on. So I guess that she really meant it, because she been looking out for me and my daughter ever since."

"She's not breaking bread because she understands your struggle. She looking out because her conscience is fucking with her about killing Nikky's dad," Tone said with aggression in his voice.

What Tone was saying had Cee-Cee feeling a certain way, but she wouldn't let Tone know it though. "Baby, where do you get these lies from?" Cee-Cee questioned.

Tone wasn't ready to confess where he had gotten his info from.

"Cee-Cee, you just gotta trust me on this."

"No, I don't have to trust you on nothing. You been gone for a minute and just pop up out the blue with a bunch of bullshit. I don't need to hear this shit, Tone. Everything been fine for me and Nikky since you been gone and I would like it to stay that way," Cee-Cee said, standing up and going to the kitchen to retrieve a bottle of Moet.

"Listen, that bitch owes me a lot of money for that last heist I pulled with Rico."

"How do Tata owe you? Because I know that she didn't help you all rob no damn jewelry store," Cee-Cee retorted.

Tone took a deep breath. He was trying hard to maintain his composure. He didn't like how Cee-Cee was being rebellious. "She owes me because she killed Rico and sold the merchandise from the jewelry heist. I want my cut of the money. Now are you gonna help me get my money from this bitch or not?"

"I don't know if I can help you do that, Tone."

"Why the fuck not?" Tone asked.

"Because Tata don't come around. When I tell her that I need something for the baby, she always send money through Cash App or through Money Gram. She never delivers money personally."

Tone just shook his head. He was feeling like it was going to be difficult to locate Tata and his money. He had to work the situation to his advantage. He knew that Cee-Cee was his only link to Tata and he had to play her to get to Tata. The whole time while he was in down in Miami, Cee-Cee had been keeping in touch with him and giving him updates on what was taking place in the city. Cee-Cee begged him to let her and Nikky come down to Miami with him, but he thought that wasn't a good idea. If the Feds got on to him down there, Cee-Cee and Nikky would have only slowed him down if he had to flee. So when she moved to her new apartment, she had texted him the new address.

Tone knew that he had to loosen Cee-Cee up. He got off the couch and retrieved the pillowcase that he had dropped on the hallway floor. Coming back, he dug in the pillowcase and removed a bundle of money and handed it to Cee-Cee. "I want you to go shopping with this for you and Nikky," Tone said, handing the money to Cee-Cee.

Cee-Cee's face lit up as she snatched the money out of Tone's hand. "OMG, baby! Thank you so much. I love you so fucking much, baby!" Cee-Cee cried out in excitement as she gave Tone a peck on the cheek. She took off to the bedroom to shower and get cleaned up so she could hit the Rodeo Drive of the East coast, where you could buy all your favorite labels like Christion Dior, Jimmy Choo, Gucci, and Louis Vuitton.

Tone shook his head once again at Cee-Cee's greediness. At that very moment, he knew he had to get the shady bitch's hooks out of his heart.

CHAPTER 15

Whip rotated through the city without a precise destination. He was just cruising though the hood to see what was popping and looking for a new location that he could place his dope down at. The work that he had gotten was an overnight success. The money was coming in constantly and he was ready to re-up and go back to the table with the dope to put his whip game down and do it all over again. Both traps were moving bundles after bundles.

The Johnny Boys takeover was a smooth transition, but that often happened when the gunplay was vicious. Whip eased the red Charger to the red light and his thoughts turned to Tata.

Tata was the epitome of a bad bitch. Whip had encountered numerous fine-ass women, but there was something about Tata that made him feel like he was a transmitter and she was on all his frequencies. Whip knew that he didn't have time to pursue a woman like Tata, but her energy had a pull on him that was undeniable. He was sure that Tata was too tied up in the streets to even notice a real nigga like him, Whip rationalized with himself. The light turned green and he pushed the Charger through the light. He bit down on his lip, thinking about how sexy and curvy Tata's body was. His manhood twitched in his jeans thinking about her soup cooler lips.

The sun was starting to set and the city was becoming dark. Whip found himself sitting on the block of Georgia and Park Road NW. His eyes studied the block of Morton Street, an open air dope strip that did numbers back in the day. But for some reason, it was open for the wannabe dope boys that never had more than a spoon of dope at one time. Whip was puzzled as to why this strip was left open and no one had claimed the block and rebirthed it. He could understand with the new changes what was taking place around this section of the city. The white people in D.C., for some reason, wanted this section of the city, and Whip knew this made it clear why it wasn't controlled and locked down by anyone.

Whip pulled an already-rolled Garcia Vega from out of his sun visor and taking a Bic lighter, he put flame to the Vega and inhaled deeply. The Loud pack filled his lungs. He watched the street with a hawk's eye. Automatically, he was mentally formulating a plan to organize and put his dope down on Morton Street. Mentally he could see the money coming in. The D.C.B. would have to move in quickly - no guns blazing, but with cleverness. Whip let a cloud of smoke out of his lungs and tapped ashes from the Vega into the car's ashtray.

The block was live. Cars were pulling up and niggas were just rushing the cars to be the first one to make the sale. It was an every man for himself strip. It didn't seem that anyone had a set clientele.

A familiar face appeared from between the buildings on Morton Street. "Bitch-ass nigga! This where your faggot ass been hiding at all this time?" Whip spoke to himself as he watched Spoon run from between the red brick buildings and run to a black van to make a dope sale. Just as quickly as he appeared, he disappeared back between the buildings.

Whip picked his phone up and hit up Racks. She didn't answer, so he shot her a quick text telling her to hit him up ASAP. Twenty minutes had passed and Spoon emerged from between the buildings again to make another sale. Whip started to get frustrated. He picked his phone up off his lap and hit Tata up.

"Hello?" Tata's sexy voice came through on the third ring.

"Tata, where the homie Racks? She ain't picking up her phone," Whip said all in one breath, still watching the cut where Spoon was ducking back off.

"Who the fuck is this?" Tata asked aggressively.

"Whip!"

"Oh, my bad, Whip, I don't know where Racks is. She probably getting some rest. We got a big day tomorrow."

"Fuck!" Whip said angrily.

Tata balled her face up on the other end of the phone. "What's good, Whip?"

"Nothing!" Whip retorted and then he hung the phone up in Tata's ear. Whip reached in the back seat and grabbed his black Howard University hoodie and a red Nationals cap. After pulling the sweat shirt on and the hat low over his eyes, Whip reached in the glove compartment and removed his gloves and red bandanna. He tied the bandanna around his neck and checked the clip of his 50 cal. Desert

Eagle. Whip puffed on the loud a few more times before he put the Vega out in the ashtray. He waited patiently to make his move.

He didn't have to wait long. Spoon made his way out of the cut to make another sale. After the transaction, he didn't go back between the buildings. He started walking up the block. Whip jumped out of the Charger and followed Spoon.

Spoon was about to meet his street justice. Spoon had failed to do his part on a caper that that got Racks' cousin Gunz killed. And to make matters worse, he left Racks for dead at the gas station, where she had to shoot it out with the police. If it wasn't for Tata, Racks would have been sitting over in D.C. jail facing murder charges or even worse. Racks could have been lying in Harmony Cemetery along with her cousin Gunz.

Whip kept his head down as he trailed Spoon, his gloved hand gripped firmly on the handle of the 50 cal. he concealed in the pouch of his sweat shirt. Even though Whip was low and his eyes were down, he could see everything that was transpiring around him. The dope boys were still rushing the cars as they rolled up to be served the block poison. A few project chicks sat on a stoop and shared a Backwood and gossiped about who had a big dick and who they wanted to give the pussy to next. Once Whip got deeper into the block, he caught a glimpse of a familiar face. And if he wasn't mistaken, the familiar face had seen him also. But he was puzzled as to why that familiar face was in the same area with Spoon. Clearly he knew this was a violation. But Whip would have to deal with that later. He had to deal with the task at hand, and that was to send Spoon away with a closed casket.

Spoon made a right around a corner at the end of the block, Whip picked his pace up. The side street they had just turned on was perfect. It was dark with a dim street lamp posted up on its corner. Spoon's phone rang and he answered. Whip eased the cannon out the hoodie pouch. He quickly scanned the porches of the houses and the cars that occupied the street. He was about to run down on Spoon's ass, but Spoon did something that Whip wasn't anticipating. Spoon spun around on his heels and banged shots from the concealed 38 special he yanked off his hip.

Spoon's shots open up the night.

"Shit!" Whip whispered as he fell. He heard the .38 bullets whiz closely past his head. Whip got low and made a dash between two parked cars. He stuck the 50 cal over the trunk of me of the cars and let it roar.

The hand cannon sounded like three sticks of dynamite were ignited. Being on the opposite end of the 50 cal. made Spoon panic. The roar and vibration from Whip's gun made Spoon's bone vibrate in his skin and just like the bitch nigga he was, he took flight.

Whip peeked his head from between the cars and saw Spoon in flight mode. He knew he had the chump where he wanted him. He raised his gun and clenched with both hands, biting down on his bottom lip. He put Spoon in his sight and pulled the trigger The Desert shrieked out, kicking hard in Whip's grip.

Spoon hollered out in pain as the 50 cal bullet drilled a hole in Spoon's hamstring, shattering his bone on contact. Spoon fell, sliding about five feet on the pavement. His phone and .38 laid a few feet in front of him. He squirmed in pain. He grabbed the back of his leg. Blood spilled between his fingers where he fought unsuccessfully to keep his blood from rushing out of the gaping hole.

Whip briskly walked up on a wounded and crying Spoon.

"Come on, Blood, don't do this shit to me, Blood," Spoon pleaded.

Whip's lip curled into a snarl. The only thing Whip hated more than a rat was a nigga that was out there living that life and when it was time to pay the debt for violating a code of the life, the first thing a muthafucka started doing was crying and pleading for his pitiful fuckin' life.

"Bitch nigga, shut the fuck up!" Whip said through clenched teeth as he walked past Spoon to retrieve Spoon's discarded gun and phone. He placed the phone and gun in his back pocket.

Spoon tried to sit up, but the greeting that Whip's red and black Foamposites gave his face forced Spoon to lay it back down. But that didn't stop him from trying to convince Whip to spare his life.

"Aye Blood!" Spoon struggled to speak through the pain in his leg and face. "Give a nigga a break, Blood. I put in on the set you'll never see my face again. Blood, just give a nigga a pass, Whip. I got a little girl that needs me," Spoon cried out. Snot shot out from his nose, causing him to look more pitiful with them coward-ass tears rolling down his face.

"What about Racks? Don't you think her cousin Gunz needs her?" Whip retorted. Whip placed his foot on Spoon's chest and pointed his gun at Spoon's head. "I'll do you a favor though, slim," Whip said.

Spoon took a deep swallow. "What's that, Blood?"

Whip smiled. "I'll let your daughter know you died crying like a bitch."

Whip pulled the trigger, caving Spoon's head in with three dome shots.

Boom, boom, boom!

A masked man stepped from between a set of houses on the block busting shots, trying to end Whip's life just like he ended Spoon's life. Whip dipped between another set of parked cars and traded shots with the gunman.

A police cruiser came around the corner out of nowhere and the gunman sent a gush of bullets through its front windshield, sending the cruiser crashing into a park car. Two more cruisers came around the corner. The masked gunman let his thirty round extended talk to them before he made it back between the houses where he came from.

Whip knew his ass had to get the fuck up outta there. There was a body on the sidewalk that he held the murder weapon to and a potential dead cop. Whip knew that was a recipe for destruction. Whip took a deep breath and sprinted from between the cars. He was familiar with the area because a few years ago, he used to hustle in front of the Madness Shop on the avenue and use to fuck a mud duck named Charity that lived down the street from the Madness Shop. A mud was a bitch with an ugly face and a straight stunner chick body.

Whip ran with everything he had in him. He had made it to the end of the block before one of the police officers driving the cruiser noticed him. They lit the cherries up and fled after him while the other cruiser aided and assisted his fallen comrade.

Whip bent the corner on Kenyon Street. His legs had already begun to burn right along with his lungs. He could hear the engine of the police cruiser roar and knew they were gaining on him. Whip breathed through his mouth. He quickly made a dash between a set of houses that put him in the alley down from Charity's house.

"Fuck!" Whip yelled out as he tripped on a rock and fell. The gun fell out of his hand. He struggled to get to his feet. He bent over towards the Desert Eagle and picked up the gun. Just then he heard a noise coming from between the houses where he had just come from. "Damn," Whip muttered.

Man's best friend wearing a K-9 unit vest came running towards him full speed. Whip moved out of instinct. He lifted the D.E. and blessed the K-9 with the wrath of his cannon. The bullets slammed into the beast's chest, stopping him in his tracks.

Whip turned and tried to run, but the pain in his ankle was too much. He made it to old man Haywood's garage. He lived two houses away from Charity. He lifted the garage door a few feet, rolled under it, and closed it back. Whip could hear voices and cars zoom up and down the alley.

An old 1979 Fleetwood Caddie sat in the garage. The car had seen better days. Mr. Haywood had a stroke and he wasn't able to drive the car anymore, so it sat in the garage rotting away with time. When Whip used to hustle in front of the Madness Shop, he use to stash his work in the old man's car. But now the car was used as a shooting gallery for the dope fiends and a place for the low price whores to turn their tricks.

Whip opened the back door and eased into the car's back seat. He was careful not to make any noise when he closed the door or when he pulled the back seat from the car frame and crawled into the trunk through the back seat.

The smell in the trunk was unbearable. Whip fought to hold the contents of his stomach. He was lying on something squishy and sticky. The more he moved around in the trunk, the more potent the odor became. It smelled like something was dead. Whip fished his phone out of his pocket and hit redial on his phone.

Tata answered the phone "Hello!"

"Aye shawty, I need you help!" Whip whispered into the phone.

After Whip gave Tata the rundown of the situation, she

immediately said she was on her way. Whip disconnected the call and hoped like hell that Tata would hurry the fuck up. Out of curiosity, Whip had to find out what the fuck he was lying in and what the odor was that was making him dizzy. He used the light from his phone to scan the Caddie trunk. Whip had to swallow his throw up several times once he saw he was lying on a litter of dead kittens.

Jibril Williams

CHAPTER 16

"Oh fuck no! You stink like shit!" Tata said, scrunching up her face and fanning her hand in front of her nose. She stared at Whip, who laid across the back seat of her truck.

"My bad, Tata, but a nigga was hiding for his fucking life. I ended up in the trunk of an abandoned car with some dead-ass cats in there," Whip retorted.

Tata pulled out of the alley on Kenyon Street. Police presence was still kind of heavy in the area, but Tata didn't have a problem easing past them. She rolled her windows down, trying to rid the truck's cabin of the foul smell that clung to Whip's body. She grabbed her strawberry air freshener and sprayed a heavy mist of it in the air. As Tata put some distance between them and the crime scene, Whip wiped his Desert Eagle down with the red bandanna that was around his neck. He sat up on the back seat and told Tata to pull over on the corner of Bryant Street. Whip opened the back door and dropped the cannon and the .38 down a storm drain. He hated to depart with the 50 cal., but he had to. Tata saw the hesitation in Whip to depart with the weapon. Whip closed the door and laid back down on the back seat.

Whip was in deep thoughts. He was trying to figure out how he was going to deal with the betrayal amongst his set. He fished Spoon's phone out of his back pocket. He was heated at what he saw. The nigga Ink had been fucking with Spoon on the low. Ink must have peeped Whip following Spoon and given Spoon a call to give him the heads up. Ink's number was the last incoming call on Spoon's phone, so the goon that was busting at him after he splacked Spoon must have been Ink. Well, that was how he put things together in his head. Whip was ready to murk Ink.

"So what the fuck happened?" Tata asked, breaking the silence in the truck, which brought Whip out of his thoughts.

"Say what?"

"What happened?" Tata asked again.

Whip thought a minute on how he was going to answer the chocolate-covered angel. Whip sat up in the truck. "I had to straighten out a nigga for a violation."

Tata was waiting on more insight, but Whip just left it at that. "I can understand that. I been there a few times myself," Tata stated, not even sure why she made the statement to Whip. She passed him a cherry-flavored Backwood and seven grams of some loud pack, which Whip gladly accepted. He twisted a fat one up. Tata watched Whip through the rearview mirror. As she was admiring how he used his tongue to seal the weed in the Backwood, a slight tingle burned between her legs. She hurried up and diverted her eyes from Whip's lips. They shared the weed back and forth between them.

By the time they made it to Tata's crib, they were nice and buzzed. Whip slightly limped behind Tata. Once they made it inside Tata's apartment, Tata stopped Whip just on the inside of the door and ordered him to strip. She went into the kitchen and came back with a plastic bag. "I'm sorry, Whip, but I can't let you in my crib smelling like that. Put them funky-ass clothes in the bag and tie it in a knot."

Whip looked at Tata as if she had two heads, but thought about it and then said, "Fuck it." He handed Tata his bifocals. He didn't look bad without his glasses. Actually, he was handsome, Tata thought. Whip pulled the hoodie and his T-shirt off at the same time. The knots in his stomach made Tata gasp. She had seen six packs before, but she never seen an eight pack in her life. She fought herself not to reach out and touch Whip's stomach.

Whip stepped out of his red and black Foamposites and his black jeans came next. He stood before Tata with nothing on but a pair of Polo boxer briefs.

"You want me to take these off too?" Whip asked with a devilish grin on his face.

"N-No!" Tata stuttered. She bent down, picking up Whip's clothes from the floor, and found herself eye level with the bulge that was pressing against the fabric of his Polo boxer briefs. Tata fumbled with putting the clothes in the bag. Once the task was done, she hurried up and straightened her back and gave Whip back his glasses. "Ummm, the bathroom is down the hall. You can find everything you need in there," Tata said, walking away to put the bag of clothes outside on her back porch. She then went to her master bedroom, where she retrieved a pair of sweatpants she had stolen from Rico's collection of sweat gear. She had the item not because it brought memories to her, but just the mere fact that she found those particular Polo sweatpants comfortable to sleep in. Tata saw something else that belonged to Rico. The chrome 45 with the crushed red diamond handle stared back at her. Her eyes roamed over the gun before she closed the drawer.

Whip had no problem finding everything he needed in Tata's bathroom. He admired how clean her bathroom was. He scrubbed himself down thoroughly with a wash cloth and some Dove body wash. His thoughts turned to Tata. "Damn, shorty fine," Whip said to himself. He saw her how eyes kept dropping down to his print and abs, so he figured there was some type of attraction there, but he wondered how would she really react if he tried his hand with her.

Whip placed his head under the shower head and let the water beat down on him. He wondered what the fuck was going on with Boot. He needed to get this nigga Boot on the line and put him on point, Whip thought, turning the water off and stepping out of the shower. He grabbed the towel off the toilet and dried the glistening water off his body. He grabbed his glasses of the counter and began drying water off his back and shoulders when Tata walk in.

"Oh shit!" Tata exclaimed, not expecting to catch Whip in the middle of drying off. She was just hoping he was still in the shower. Her intention was to creep in and put the sweatpants on the toilet and ease back out. But things didn't go as planned. So now she was getting an eyeful of Whip's king-ding-a-ling.

Frozen with the towel over his shoulders, Whip watched Tata take him in and all he could do was smirk.

"Umm, this is for you," Tata said, handing Whip the Polo sweats. She immediately left the bathroom, embarrassed as hell.

Whip put the sweats on. They were a little too big, but he couldn't complain.

He found Tata in the kitchen pouring a glass of Moscato. The way that her black Red Robin jeans were glued to her hips and hugged her curves made Whip want to get lost in her touch. She stepped out of her Red Bottoms and took a sip of her Moscato.

Watching Tata from behind, Whip took in her 5'7" height and how her thick backside sat nicely on her back.

"Trust me, my face is prettier than my ass. Are you just going to stare or come have a drink with me?" Tata stated, looking over her shoulder at a shirtless Whip.

"My bad for staring, shorty."

"No, don't apologize we even now. I didn't mean to stare earlier."

They both shared a laugh.

"You asked me to have drink with you, but I'm gonna need something stronger than that," Whip implied, nodding to the Moscato Tata was drinking.

Turning her back to Whip, Tata bent over at the waist, giving Whip a good clear view her backside. She opened the cabinet under the sink and removed a bottle of Hennessy Black.

"Okay, that's what a Blood talking about!"

"What you getting excited about, the Henny or my ass?"

"Both!" Whip replied.

"Whip, you are a mess," Tata stated, giggling. She found a glass in the cabinet and poured Whip a drink. For some reason, she felt comfortable with Whip. The only thing that threw her off about the goon was the thick-ass bifocal glasses that he wore.

Tata handed the glass of Henny to Whip. He denied the glass and grabbed the whole bottle of Hennessy Black and took a drink from the bottle.

"Okay!" Tata said, walking past Whip. "Your phone is on the table. I'm going to take a quick shower. There's some loud pack in the glass candy bowl on the table in the living room next to your phone," Tata said, disappearing down the hall.

Whip watched Tata's ass oscillate from side to side as she disappeared down the hallway. He shook his head and grabbed his dick through his sweatpants. He took a gulp of the brown liquid and made his way to the living room to find his phone and Tata's personal stash of loud pack. His twisted up a Backwood and dialed Boot's number. The phone rang three times before it went to voicemail. He hit Racks up and her phone went to voicemail on the first ring. Becoming concerned, he sent Boot and Racks texts telling them to check in with him ASAP.

Whip turned the TV on, hit the power button on the PS3, and

grabbed the controller off the table. He was feeling Tata. He had never been over at a woman's crib that had Call of Duty Black Ops on standby. He sat on the edge of the table as if he lived there and played the game.

Twenty minutes later, Tata stepped in the living room in a gray lace thong. Her luscious ass ate the thong up. The silk see through T-shirt she wore was tight and her erect nipples could be clearly seen through the material. The dark outline of her areolas was a sight for sore eyes. The material was so thin it was as if she was shirtless. She had her hair in a ponytail and a thin layer of MAC lip gloss on her bubble lips. Tata walked up behind an unaware Whip and tapped him up the shoulder with the chrome fo'-fifth she held in her hand.

"You look comfortable," Tata said, interrupting his game.

The cold steel on Whip's back and the sudden presence of Tata made him jump a little. Seeing Tata standing over him half-naked and clutching the burner made him see her in a whole new light.

"There's nothing sexier than a bad-ass boss bitch clutching a gun," Whip said, pulling on the Backwood.

Tata handed him the gun and straddled his lap. The sudden move had Whip puzzled. He didn't know that Tata was the aggressive type.

"I could tell that you didn't want to depart with the Desert. This not as big as the Desert, but it will get the job done and it's just as pretty as me."

Whip turned the gun over in his hand, examining the tool and the red diamonds that rested in its handle. "This me right here all day? Are you sure that you want me to have it?"

"Yeah, if you want it."

Whip laid the gun down on the floor by his foot. "What about these?" Whip asked, taking Tata's B-cups into his hands and giving them a slight squeeze.

Tata had been craving to be touched. Seeing Whip's big ole dick had her acting a fool.

"They can be yours as well," Tata said sexually, kissing Whip's lips.

Whip hungrily accepted Tata's kiss, exploring her lips and tongue with his. He sucked greedily on Tata's bottom lip. He slipped a hand over her soft butt and gave it a firm squeeze. Tata welcomed Whip's touch by positioning herself on Whip's dick that was pushing against his sweatpants and grinding on him. The touching and kissing were intense between them. Neither one of them wanted to rush. The sudden chemistry they shared made them want to take it slow.

Tata dragged her mint green-colored nails over Whip's chiseled back as she fed him her tongue. Whip worked a hand under Tata, finding her middle piece. Pushing her thong to the side, he inserted his middle finger into her all the way to his knuckle

"Ssssssss!" Tata let out a moan when Whip's finger penetrated her.

Whip expertly swirled his finger around Tata's opening. Her tightness clung firmly to his finger. Whip took his thumb and worked Tata's clit with it, making small circular motions while applying some light pressure.

"Ooooh!" Tata moaned in Whip's mouth. The maneuver proved to be dramatic for Tata because she removed her lips from Whip's and blurted out in ecstasy, "Oh shit, papi, give me another finger. Put another one in this pussy!"

Whip obliged Tata's request and inserted another finger in her tightness. Tata's center piece was rubber band tight around his fingers. Whip worked his fingers in and out of Tata in a hula hoop fashion while still entertaining her love button. He got excited seeing Tata's eyes squeeze shut. She was rocking a mean fuck face.

Tata rocked back and forth on his fingers, loving the sensation that he was sending through her body. Tata's pussy was so overwhelmed with juices that Whip could feel her essence leak and drip down his knuckles.

"Oh papi, don't stop, I'm cumming, papi. I'm cumming, papi," Tata said, breathing heavily. Tata shuddered on Whip's lap and fingers.

He looked down and saw his fingers coated with a thick white substance. He didn't want to do anything else but be inside Tata.

Whip pulled his fingers out of Tata and placed them in his mouth. He loved the way that pussy tasted. Tata's saltiness had him ready to pound her guts out. Tata stood up and pulled her lace thong down to her ankles and stepped out of them, giving Whip a close up of her landing strip-shaved pussy. Whip stood up and dropped his sweatpants. Tata look down at his thick long pipe and knew she might've jumped all the way out there with Whip. She was too tight to be taking all that dick.

Tata kissed Whip again. She found him to be a great kisser. She took ahold of his miniature meat bat and stroked him steadily, loving the thickness in her hands. Gripping Tata's soft body, Whip pulled the silk material of the shirt over Tata's head, letting her bare breasts fall against his chest. Whip backed Tata up against couch, where she lowered herself onto it and parted her legs so Whip could take his position between them. Whip got over Tata in a push up position. Tata rubbed her hand up and down Whip's chest and abs.

"Papi, your body is a work of God," Tata said while she worked the head of his dick up and down the slit of her opening. Tata's nipples were budded.

Whip felt the wetness and heat from Tata's love box on the tip of his throbbing manhood. He wasn't ready to enter Tata yet. He wanted to lock Tata down. He planted small kisses on Tata's forehead. He patiently and skillfully worked his kisses down to her perfect chocolate nipples. He softly sucked each budded nipple. Whip could feel Tata's body respond. Tata gripped the back of Whip's head, encouraging him on.

"Ahhh! Whip, yes, papi!" Tata hissed.

Whip moved down her stomach, dragging his tongue across her flesh, leaving behind a moist trail that stopped at the soft lips of her pussy. Whip ran his tongue up and down between Tata's folds, tasting her honey straight from the honey pot.

"Oooh, Whip! Oh, papi, please!" Tata begged as his tongue made contact with her creases.

Whip tongue danced over Tata's clitoris, dictating to her to arch her back in anticipation. Seeing how sensitive Tata was under his tongue, he latched onto Tata's clit and sucked it vigorously. Once Tata's body began to twitch uncontrollably, Whip placed the same two fingers back into her slick tunnel.

"Mmmm, papi, please stop!" Tata passionately cried out.

But Whip ignored her cry and continued to push and slide his fingers in and out of her as he still had her clit captured.

"Oh fuck, papi, I'm cumming again!" Tata announced as she palmed the back of Whip's head like a basketball and her body jerked with every tender lick Whip gave her.

The way Tata keep calling Whip "papi" had him fucked up and ready to get in her guts. Whip broke free of Tata's basketball grip and repositioned himself between Tata's thighs with his solid meat bat aimed directly at her quivering pussy. He was ready to give Tata that thug loving that was straight pressure. He pushed himself deep into Tata and he instantly felt her muscles contract around his dick.

"Whip, you feel so good inside of me, papi," Tata stated in a childlike tone. She started to gyrate her hips rhythmically.

He could tell Tata was trying to get used to his size so he just rocked back and forth into her. It didn't take long for her to get used to Whip's size because she threw a leg over the back of the couch.

"Get this pussy. Fuck me good, Whip."

Whip grinned as he got up in a push up position and slammed his meaty ten inch bat into her.

"Oh shit, papi!"

Tata tried to run from the dick, but Whip wasn't having that. Once he got Tata's head pinned against the arm rest of the couch, it was a wrap. He started serving Tata that pressure. Thap-thap-thap was the sound their bodies made when they clashed together.

"Oh, hold up. Papi, my stomach," Tata cried out, feeling Whip all the way in her guts.

Whip didn't slow his roll. He focused on how Tata's breasts bounced when he was slamming into her. His manhood was cover in her clear sticky juices and that only excited Whip, making him speed up his thrusts.

"This me right here, huh? Keep calling me papi. This my pussy, huh?" Whip asked, trying to put claim on the beautiful diva. Good pussy had a tendency to do this to a nigga.

But before Tata could give her answer, a knock at the door interrupted their fuck session.

CHAPTER 17

Hearing the knock at the door forced Tata's hand to shoot to Whip's chest, stopping him in mid-stroke. Once she heard the knock again, she immediately pushed Whip out of her wetness. It gave off a gushy sound.

"Oh shit!" Tata said.

"What?" Whip replied, hopping up and picking the fo'-fifth up off the floor.

"Don't no one know where I live except my girls, and they always call before they come to my crib," Tata said, tiptoeing to the door. Whip hurried up and stepped back into his sweat pants. Tata peeked out the peephole and her eyes got big. "Fuck!" she whispered. She ran back into the living room to place her thong back on along with her thin shirt.

"Who's at the door?" Whip asked, checking the fo'-fifth for bullets and finding it was fully loaded. He jacked a bullet in the chambers.

"It's Zoey and Racks!"

"Well, open the door," Whip said in confusion. He didn't know why Tata was acting all weird all of sudden.

"We can't be seen like this!" Tata stated, taking off to her room.

Tata's statement had Whip in his bag. He really didn't know how to take the statement. But the way that she said it made him feel a certain way. Tata came back out of her room wearing a pair of sky blue sweatpants with the word "juicy" on the back of them. She had traded her silky thin T- shirt for a white wife beater.

Another knock came across the door. "I'm coming!" Tata shouted. She looked over at Whip, who now was sitting on the couch smoking another Backwood with the fo'-fifth resting across his lap.

Tata opened the door. "What the fuck you want and why you didn't call before you came through here?" Tata questioned.

"Damn, mami, sorry, I forgot to call and - " Zoey stopped talking once she walked in Tata's apartment and saw Whip sitting on the couch smoking a Backwood. Tata couldn't make eye contact with Zoey.

"Suuwoo!" Racks said to Whip, seeing him sitting on the couch. She threw up her B's and Whip returned the gang sign.

Zoey looked at Whip then back at Tata. Tata still hadn't made eye contact with her. Tata closed the door behind her unexpected guests.

Zoey wondered why Whip was shirtless and laid up in Tata's crib until the faint scent hit her nose. "Un-uh! It smells like pussy in here. You muthafuckas been in here fuckin'," Zoey blurted out, embarrassing the shit out of Tata.

"Girl, shut the fuck up. It don't smell like nothing in here but strawberry air freshener and loud pack."

"Shiiid, if strawberry air freshener smells like that, then I won't never spray that shit in my crib," Zoey said sarcastically, tooting her nose up, making Tata feel a little self-conscious about if her pussy had an odor to it or not.

Racks found this amusing. She busted out laughing. "Tata, don't pay Zoey no mind. That what good pussy supposed to smell like." Racks continued to laugh and grab the crotch of her pants like she was a dude.

"Fuck you bitches, and wasn't nobody in here fucking. The question is, where you two bitches been?"

"We hit a movie," Zoey retorted.

"Aye Racks, I been blowing your line up. Why you ain't pick up?" Whip asked.

"Fuck! My bad, Blood. I went in the movies and turned my phone off," Racks said, pulling her phone out of her pocket and turning it on. Instantly her phone began chiming, alerting her she had all type of notifications pending. She immediately started jumping up and down once she checked her Facebook account and saw the latest topic that was posted. "Oh shit, someone finally murked that nigga Spoon," Racks said, throwing her B's up in the air.

Whip didn't comment on the news that Racks conveyed to him. Zoey just watched in awe how excited her friend was about the death of Spoon. Racks had given her the full rundown on Spoon and how he got her cousin killed. Zoey pulled a sour apple Blow Pop out of her back pocket, snatched the wax wrapper off it, and sucked it in her mouth.

Tata watched Whip and his nonchalant demeanor told her this was the violation he was speaking about earlier tonight.

"Aye Racks, you got some extra shoes and a T-shirt in your car?" Whip asked.

"You know that I do. You never know when you got to switch it up," Racks replied.

"Well, go grab me a pair shoes and shirt so we can bounce. We gotta find Boot. He ain't answering his phone either. I got to lace you and him up on something."

Racks read the serious body language that Whip was giving up. She dipped to go grab the things Whip needed out of her car. Racks came back with a pair of red and black Air Max's. He and Racks wore the same size. He had no problem putting his feet in the shoes. Whip then pulled a black T-shirt over his head. He was ready to go. He tucked the burner Tata gave him in his waistline. He looked at Tata for any sign they would hook up another time, but Tata didn't make eye contact with him.

"Aye, hit my line, Tata," Whip said.

"A'ight!" Tata said, pouring herself a drink.

Zoey watched the exchange between Whip and Tata. She could tell that she was having regrets about fucking Whip, but she didn't know why. Whip and Racks left and Zoey locked the door behind them.

"You want to talk about it, mami?" Zoey asked.

"Nope! Just keep the situation between us for now," Tata instructed.

"Like Alicia Keys, your secrets are safe with me."

Tata rolled her eyes at her friend's silly-ass statement. Zoey was the type that always found the wrong shit to say at the wrong time.

Tata's phone rang. Seeing that it was Cee-Cee calling, she started to ignore the call, but she changed her mind and hit the talk button.

"What's good, mami?" Tata asked.

"Ain't nothing, girl. I just called to spill some tea. Girl, they just found Diesel shot the fuck up in his apartment."

The news was kinda shocking to Tata. She truly thought that she and Billie had sent Diesel's bitch ass on a dirt nap over a week ago.

This mistake could have cost her and her team their lives or freedom. Next time she moved on her nemesis, she was going to make sure it was all head shots.

"Damn, that's fucked up! Did they say who did it?" Tata inquired.

"Naw, don't nobody know shit. But look, is everything still a go on the move?" Cee-Cee asked, hoping that Tata say yeah.

"Everything is everything, but look, I got company right now so I will chop it up with you later. And keep me informed if you hear anything else about Diesel."

"Okay, I will," Cee-Cee stated, disconnecting the call.

*****

"What's on your mind, big homie?" Racks asked, looking at Whip, who was riding shotgun with his mind in deep thought as the scenery floated by him.

Whip came out of his trance and pushed his bifocals back farther on his nose. "A whole lot, but nothing a hard lesson can't fix and place things back in their proper perspective," Whip stated flatly.

Racks' Delta 88 eased in front of Boot's crib.

The house wasn't bad looking, but it was small and the Sheriff Road neighborhood had seen better days. Boot's Dodge Durango sat in front of the house.

"What this nigga on?" Whip mumbled to himself. He couldn't figure out why Boot hadn't answered his phone if he was at the crib this whole time. He was definitely about to find out.

Whip and Racks made their way to Boot's door and Racks gave it three knocks. Moments later, Boot snatched the door open covered in sweat and accompanied with a fo'-fifth and his red nose pit name Wicked One.

"Damn, nigga, I been blowing your line up," Whip barked.

"My bad, Blood. I dropped my phone. I got to slide past T-Mobile in the morning and get me a new one," Boot retorted, turning away from the door and walking back into the living room. Wicked One trotted behind him.

This was the first time that Whip and Racks noticed that Boots was ass naked. They both shook their heads at Boot's wild ass. Once they made it to the living room, they understood why Boot was naked and covered in sweat. A chubby chick was lying on the love seat naked. She jumped when Whip and Racks walked in the room behind Boot. Boots stepped into a pair of jeans.

"A'ight, shawty, you got to bounce," Boot told his naked guest.

You could tell that she didn't like what she was hearing because she sucked her teeth loudly and aggressively started putting on her clothes. "Are you going to take me home?" she asked.

"Bitch, you better call a fucking Uber or some shit!" Boot barked.

The chick looked at him like she wanted to protest his demand, but decided not to play herself. "You know what, Boot? The next time you need some company, call one of your other bitches loose, my fucking nigga," the chick said, storming out of the house. All Whip could do was chuckle.

"So what it is, boss?" Boot spoke through clouds of smoke from the Newport that he just lit.

"I finally caught up with that nigga Spoon tonight. I pushed his hairline all the way the fuck back," Whip said.

This news brought joy to Racks' murderous heart. She knew that Whip always had her back.

"But that shit ain't about nothing," Whip continued. "The real problem is that a nigga from our organization tried to kill me."

Jibril Williams

CHAPTER 18
The next day

Nick Mayhew had been securing and protecting Bank of America money for over twenty-five years. Working for the branch had proven to be very beneficial. Nick had a beautiful four-bedroom house on the outskirts of Oxion Hill Maryland, where his loving wife Karen was a full time housewife. Karen nicknamed the house their piece of Heaven on Earth. The 2020 Buick she drove she dubbed her cruise ship because when she drove it, the automobile felt like it was floating.

Nick looked over on the other side of the armored truck and smiled at his twenty-four-year-old Curtis. At the age of fifty-seven, Nick was a proud father. He loved Curtis more than he loved the woman that birthed Curtis. Nick's son had just gotten back off a two year tour from overseas.

Nick had helped his son land a job with the bank and called in some favors and got Curtis on the same route with him. He even had the privilege of training Curtis for the last three weeks. Today was a special day for them both. Curtis would be starting on his one year probation term and today was Nick's last day riding on the Bank of America rig. He was retiring after today. He and Karen were planning on spending a few weeks in Vegas. Nick was looking forward to trying his hand on the craps table while Karen tried her luck on the slot machines.

"To all available units, we just received a potential bomb threat at four District of Columbia schools. Be advised if you are near schools Harriet Tubman, Raymond Elementary, Wilson High School, and Roosevelt High, please assist," the dispatcher's voice echoed through the rig's scanner.

Nick couldn't believe that some maniac had exposed some poor innocent children to potential danger. He wondered what the fuck the world was coming to. He thought with Donald Trump being in the White House people would stop doing barbaric shit and focus on making America great again. But it was wishful thinking on Nick's behalf.

Curtis watched his dad's face and knew the news the police

scanner conveyed had his old man thinking. Their matching blue eyes met and Curtis mouthed "last day", which made his dad feel that he was one day away from all the world's madness and getting lucky on them Vegas craps tables.

The Bank of America rig turned on South Capital Street and pulled up to the front of the bank.

"How we looking, Joe?" Nick yelled to the rig's driver.

Joe and Nick had been friends for years. They had met on the job. The two men took a liking to each other and they had been friends ever since.

"It's all clear!" Joe yelled through the small rectangle slot that separated the driver and its cargo.

"Be back in ten, Frank!" Nick stated to the pot-bellied co-worker that he wasn't too fond of due to the fact one night while Nick hosted a card game at his house, he caught the old bastard eyeing his wife Karen.

Nick grabbed a black money bag and unbolted the back door of the rig. Curtis grabbed another bag and followed his dad out of the rig. Frank secured the truck door behind them.

The morning chill hit Nick's white wrinkled face. His hand firmly gripped the butt of the Glock 17. He quickly scanned the street. He didn't pick up on any threat, so he made his way into the bank with his son.

Neither one of them had a clue that they were in the line of fire of a deadly weapon.

*****

The robbers watch the armored truck come to a halt in front of the bank. They watched the truck like welfare recipients would watch the mailbox for their first of the month check. All that could be heard in their stolen truck was the cocking of their weapons.

Cop killer ammo rested in the clips of their guns, ready to execute the robbers' deadly wrath. Suppressors were being attached to the end of each weapon with a gloved hand. The first part of their plan had been put in motion with a fake bomb threat being called in to the D.C.

public schools. The robbers wanted to draw attention away from their target to make the job easier to pull off. Now all the robbers were waiting on the green light to go in and get that paper.

*****

"How you doing today, Ce'Anna?" Nick asked the bank manager. He always was very pleasant with Ce'Anna Hightower. They had grown to know one another over the last four years.

"Hmm, I'm do-I'm doing fine," Ce'Anna stuttered as she opened the counting room vault.

This was where they counted the large sums of money. Today Nick was bringing in new bills from the Federal Reserve to switch out with the old bills that had been taken out of circulation. Ce'Anna was scheduled to have a long day ahead of her. Since she was bank manager, she was responsible for counting the half a million that Nick just dropped off.

Nick and his son placed the money bags on the counter in the counting room and grabbed the two bags that contain the out of circulation bills. They would be dropping the bills off at the Federal Reserve as the end of their route and the Federal Reserve would have the old bills burned and destroyed.

"What the fuck!" Nick said, frowning his face up. "These bags are twice as heavy as the bags we just brought in," a complaining Nick stated, switching the bag to his good hand, which was his shooting hand.

"I gotcha, Pops. You getting old on me." Curtis chuckled and grabbed the bag from his dad, embarrassing his dad in front of Ce'Anna.

"Well, your mother don't think I'm getting old," Nick retorted, hiking the front of his pants up, giving the group the implication that he'd handling business in the bedroom. Now it was Curtis's time to be embarrassed.

"Come on, Dad! That's too much info," Curtis complained, his face turning beet red.

The trio exited the counting room while Ce'Anna secured the

vault behind them.

Ce'Anna tapped a few buttons on her Apple phone watch and led the way out the back of the bank. Her Jimmy Choo's clicked against the marble floor, which enticed Nick to check out her backside. Her round rump made his manhood twitch. Nick had never been with a black woman before in his life but if he could, he would want his experience to be with a black strapped like Ce'Anna. Some of his old buddies had the pleasure of sleeping with black women and they always said the same thing: "Once you go black, you never go back."

Reaching the bank counter, Ce'Anna turned on her heels, catching Nick's eyes glued to her ass.

"You thought I forgot that today was your last day, huh?"

"Well, my last day is nothing to be excited about," Nick said, stepping from behind the banks counter.

Four Metropolitan police officers stormed the bank. The leading officer tapped the trigger on the Glock. No sound came from the weapon. Fire was the only thing that erupted from it. One single bullet struck the bank security guard in his neck. He fell to the floor in pain.

Another officer squeeze the trigger on the Mack 11. The suppressors on the weapon gave a phuuff-phuuff sound. Two bullets hit Nick center mass in the chest, dropping him. Nick's body folded over on the bank's floor.

Ce'Anna screamed. Curtis's military training kicked in, but he was too slow on drawing his issued Glock 17 due to him having both of his hands full with the money bags. A slug barreled through his hip, knocking him to his knees, and another bullet slam into his arm. "

"Agghhh!" Curtis let out a scream.

"Hit the fucking floor one!" of the officers said, jumping on the bank counter. He instructed the bank tellers to back up from their work stations and get on the floor.

The small crowd in the bank complied with the robbers. Everyone was face down kissing the bank's floor.

"I want all phones out in front of you," another robber instructed.

Ce'Anna was screaming and crying on the floor.

"Bitch, shut the fuck up!" the robber wearing the all-white Red Bottoms stated. She gave Ce'Anna a kick to the ribs, shutting her up.

The robbers wore clear plastic masks over their face, the kind that made it hard to see their true identity. Once the bank was 100 percent under their control, one of the robbers positioned herself by the bank's front door.

The robber with the black Red Bottoms on held down the fort on top of the counter, overseeing the whole bank. "Four minutes!" she yelled out, which sent the other two robbers into action.

One robber stepped over a bleeding Nick. She could hear the old man wheezing. Remembering the mistake she made with Diesel, she popped Nick in the head with a slug, sending him to everlasting sleep. She bent down and removed his weapon from his holster. She went over to Curtis, and her Red Bottoms click-clacked along the way. Curtis held his hip with both hands despite the hole that he had in his forearm. He was trying his best to stop the blood that poured out of him. The robber stood over him. They made eye contact. The robber's mask was foggy from the hot air that was coming through the nostril hole of her mask. The robber slightly shook her head and squeezed the trigger on her Mack 11. The silenced weapon jerked in her latex-gloved hands.

Curtis's head banged and shattered against the bank floor. A portion of his head popped off, exposing brain matter that looked like matted worms. The robber let the Mack 11 hang from her shoulder strap that was around her neck and grabbed the two money bags that rested beside Curtis's dead body. She carried the bags to the front door, where one of the robbers held post.

The robber wearing the blue Red Bottoms dragged Ce'Anna to each teller station and made her empty the drawers.

"Two minutes!" the robber on the counter yelled.

Ce'Anna was emptying out the last teller's drawer. She was furious and shaken badly. The robber who dragged the bags to the front door began to collect the customers' phones.

"Time!" the robber with the black Red Bottoms shouted.

All the robbers met at the door. The robber that held the position by the front door grabbed the money bags. The last remaining robber scanned the bank floor, looking for anyone that wanted to play hero.

"How we looking out there, mama?" one of the robbers said

through an earpiece.

"Bring that ass on!" a voice came back through her earpiece.

"Alright, stay the fuck on the floor for five minutes. Anyone come out this bank gonna end up like these dead muthafuckas that we leaving in this bitch. Be grateful it's not you that we leaving in here stankin'. And remember, a hero is nothing but a sandwich."

On that note, the robbers made their way out of the bank with a half million dollars.

*****

Cain was sitting at his breakfast table reading the *Washington Post*. He was reading how the all-female bank robbers got away with an undisclosed amount of money and that neither the police nor the Feds had a person of interest at that time.

"Damn, them some bad-ass bitches," Cain said to himself as he took a sip of his morning coffee.

His iPhone vibrated on the table. He checked his diamond bezel AMP big head watch, and the expensive time piece read 9:15 a.m. He grabbed his phone as it danced around on the table. He was going to ignore the call, but he saw that it was his connect. It puzzled him as to what Weedy wanted so damn early in the morning. He tapped the speaker icon on the phone and Weedy's voice came through the phone.

"Cain, my man. How you doing?"

Cain set the phone on the table. "All is well, but why you ringing my line so early in the A.M.? I haven't even had my cup of coffee yet," Cain stated, folding the morning paper and taking another sip of coffee.

"The family back home wanted me to touch base with you. They already deposited three mill into your account. The rest of the money will be delivered to you in cash."

Cain already knew the money was deposited in his account yesterday when he got notice from his offshore accountant.

"I seen it, Weedy," Cain said with a little frustration in his voice because he never gave the Canadian Mob his account info. But at the same time, he admired the Mob's thoroughness. "When will I be getting the remainder of the money?" Cain asked.

"That's why I'm calling. The family wants to know what position you going to play."

"What you mean?" Cain asked, taking another sip of his coffee.

"They want to know if you going to run point for them and if not, they want to send someone down so you can show them the ins and outs of the operation and the city," Weedy stated.

Cain wasn't happy about this. "So I can't get the remainder of my money unless I either join forces with you or allow some muthafucka to come down and check my shit out?"

"That's the gist of it." Weedy let out a sigh.

Cain gave out his own sigh. "I still got a little over a month before I hand over my city. I will let you know then what I'm going to do the week I walk away. But right now, I feel like you soft pressing me," Cain said, disconnecting the call, hanging up on Weedy.

Cain sat back in his chair and thought about this situation. He knew in his heart that he could not be a puppet for the Canadian Mob, but at the same time, he was having second thoughts about handing over D.C. to them cold dick muthafuckas. Many muthafuckas wanted D.C. for political reasons, but what a nigga didn't know was D.C.'s political officials didn't support the drug dealers in any manner. And the Canadian Mob would find that out the hard way. Cain shook his head and took another sip of his coffee.

Jibril Williams

CHAPTER 19
The next morning

Tata and her Red Bottom Squad sat around her living room. There was a cold silence in the room. $500,000 of untraceable cash was piled on the living room floor. Six pair of eyes stared at the money.

"Damn, the Red Bottom Squad be getting it in," Racks said in amazement.

"Ain't no question about it. You think this something, wait until you see the next lick," Zoey said, popping a cherry-flavored Blow Pop in her mouth and wrapping her tongue around the delicious candy.

"I'm not even gonna lie. I didn't think the bitch Cee-Cee had it in her to set this shit up," Phatmama chimed in.

Before Tata could reply to Phatmama's comment, Jelli interrupted. "Tata, what the fuck was that in the bank? You just walked in that bitch straight murdering shit. You killed them guards like they were fucking dogs. We haven't been murdering on the other jobs, so why now?" Jelli asked.

Tata's brown eyes glowed a shade darker. Jelli's question angered her.

"Do you think you are better fit to lead this squad?" Tata questioned Jelli in a challenging tone.

Billie and Racks were the newest members of the group. They looked on in confusion because they thought the group was tighter than what they were displaying at the moment. But apparently there was something brewing between Tata and Jelli.

"I didn't say that. But we taking too many risks and as a leader, you should know that."

"Bitch, I'm tired of you complaining about how I move this team forward. Either you get the fuck in line or get the fuck outta line," Tata said with venom in her words and fire in her eyes.

Jelli immediately took offense at how Tata was talking to her and as always, her emotions got the best of her. "Tata, you talking like a bitch in here your muthafuckin' flunky and you and I both know I ain't never been that! You can give me my cut of the money so I can get the fuck on about my business. I was planning on breaking off from this reckless-ass group because all you gonna do is get us locked the fuck up!"

"Hold up, Jelli!" Zoey cried out.

"Naw, let her go. She's the weak link in the group anyway. If she wants out, then so be it. But know this, Jelli: once you gone, don't come back," Tata said, standing up and removing $75,000 from the stacks of money on the table and handing it to Jelli.

Tata's eye locked with Jelli's. Tata's eyes held no remorse in them. Jelli's eyes misted over. Jelli snatched the stacks of C-notes out of Tata's hand and shoved them in her Coach bag. She made eye contact with Phatmama and then Jelli's tears dropped down her cheeks. Jelli walked out of Tata's apartment, not looking back.

Billie and Racks looked on like "what the fuck just happened?"

"Tata, go get that girl!" Zoey said, getting upset about the whole ordeal. The group had been tight over the years so it was strange to see how power and money made the friendship shift.

"I'm not chasing that bitch. She wanted out, then fuck her. We got money to get, not cater to a scary-ass bitch! I told you once before if we going to survive in this game, we got to have the heart of a fucking savage," Tata said, breathing hard.

Zoey hopped off the floor and left the apartment to catch Jelli. Tata rolled her eyes at Zoey. Tata gave the rest of the group their breakdown of the money. "Racks, in one day I need you to handle something for me," Tata said, handing Racks her cut of the money.

"A'ight, just hit my line," Racks retorted.

The ladies left, leaving Phatmama and Tata behind.

"You know that you wrong for how you handled Jelli," Phatmama stated.

"Phatmama, I'm not trying to hear that right now. I'm going to call Jelli's ass later, but I can't have this shit clouding my thoughts. We need to meet Rau'f and trade the ZALES merch in for cash."

"A'ight, but make sure that you call her. You and her definitely need to have a conversation," Phatmama said, grabbing her portion of the money and her strap off the floor.

CHAPTER 20

Zoey couldn't catch Jelli in time. By the time she made it out of Tata's apartment, Jelli was gone. She pushed her Audi truck through the light D.C. traffic. She was frustrated at what took place between Tata and Jelli. Those bitches was tripping. She couldn't understand why Tata had become so damn cold. Zoey didn't know if it was the murder of Rico or the crazy-ass shootout they had at the cemetery, but the bitch Tata was definitely on one.

Zoey pulled a pre-rolled Backwood from her truck's ashtray and sparked the leaf. She took a toke of the Backwood. The diesel Kush instantly started to mellow her out.

Zoey made a right off Florida Avenue onto Georgia Avenue. When she passed the McDonald's on the left, seeing the fast food place made her stomach growl. She realized that she hadn't eaten at all today. Robbing banks and watching muthafuckas get their heads blown off yesterday had killed her appetite. Zoey whipped her truck into the McDonald's parking lot and navigated the truck to the drive thru. She pulled up behind a white Lexus.

"Damn, that joint tight," Zoey spoke to herself as she admired the Lex from the back.

Suddenly Zoey got a feeling that she had seen the car before. Taking another pull of the Backwood, Zoey searched her brain on where she had seen the car before. Staring into the Lex through its back windshield, she could tell that the car was occupied by two people, a male and female. Zoey rolled down her window and flicked ashes from her Backwood out the window. The Lexus eased up to the intercom to place its order. A church van pulled in behind her, blocking her in.

When the driver of the Lex leaned out his window and started riffing off his order, Zoey's heart started beating fast, causing her blood to shoot though her body at a rocket speed.

She sat up in her seat, trying to get a better look at the driver. But before she could get a better look, the driver pulled his head back into the car. "Shit!" Zoey said out loud to herself. The Lex moved up to the window to pick up and pay for his order. It was Zoey's turn to order.

She eased the truck up to the intercom with her eyes still glued to the back of the Lex

"Welcome to McDonald's, may I take your order?" a voice happily came through the intercom.

Suddenly Zoey wasn't hungry anymore. Her inquisitiveness consumed her appetite. "Ummm, I'm sorry, I changed my mind. I don't want to eat here," Zoey said into the intercom.

"Okay, no problem," the voice came through the intercom, but Zoey could clearly hear the annoyance in the woman voice.

But Zoey wasn't concerned with the minimum wage worker's attitude.

*****

"Tata, nice to be seeing you again," Rau'f said, kissing her on both cheeks.

"Nice seeing you," Tata said, taking a seat in one of Rau'f's plush chairs and crossing her thick legs.

Rau'f admired her thickness briefly before he went and took a seat behind his desk. "Before we start, I want to give you my condolences about Rico. I know that must been hard to bury him," Rau'f stated, picking a cigar up out of the crystal ashtray and taking a pull from it.

Tata needed Rau'f to take her seriously. She knew that it would only be a matter of time before he grew tired of her. It was in every man's nature to try a woman that was eating in a man's game. So she locked eyes with Rau'f. "What you think was harder? Me killing Rico, or me burying his ass?"

Tata's bluntness made Rau'f fumble his cigar. The cigar bounced on the glass desk. Rau'f snatched it up quickly and knocked the ashes from the cigar onto the floor. Tata loved the reaction she got from him, but she didn't dare smile.

Rau'f's eyes went to his security monitors. "Who's your friend? That's not the same lovely face that you brought with you the last time that you came to see me," Rau'f questioned Tata. He was inquiring about Phatmama, who was browsing through his Lexus dealership, but she cautiously kept her eye on the door she saw Tata disappear through moments ago.

"That's my right hand. I was hoping that you could have met with her today. Her name is Phatmama," Tata stated, uncrossing and re-crossing her legs.

"Nice!" Rau'f mumbled. "Maybe next time. But right now, I think we should move on with business." Rau'f turned his attention from the monitors back to Tata.

Tata reached down and removed the knapsack that was resting next to her chair. She handed it to Rau'f. Rau'f opened the knapsack and began placing jewelry piece after jewelry piece on a black velvet cloth that rested on the top of his glass desk. Tata took in the office and just like the last time that she was there, she couldn't help the feeling that she was surrounded by money. She knew that the glass desk Rau'f worked from was worth a check, but nothing in the room really screamed money except Rau'f himself.

Rau'f pulled a slew of diamond rings from the bag and placed them on the black velvet. The Cartier collection came next. He removed five Cartier watches of various sizes. Once Rau'f was finish emptying out the bag, he focused mostly on the Rolexes, the two white gold Daytona's and the Oyster Perpetual Air King with the black diamond bezels. The Tank Anglaise was Tata's favorite. She wanted to keep the watch so bad, but she couldn't risk keeping the watch for herself. It was bad enough that she was selfishly keeping the nine black diamonds. Rau'f's desktop looked like it was dripping with ice.

Rau'f smiled. He knew that Tata was something special. Most women would have started passing out the merchandise or started selling it to the corner hustlers, but not this chocolate beauty. She was calculated and about her paper. Rau'f picked up one of the diamond tennis bracelets. He immediately thought about his mistress Esther.

Tata watch Rau'f in silence. She watched how he went over every piece of jewelry. He didn't take nearly as long as the last· time she was here.

"250!" Rau'f blurted out, breaking the silence and looking up at Tata.

"I was thinking 275 at the least," Tata countered, trying to get more out of the deal.

Rau'f looked at Tata sternly. He ran a hand down his goatee. "Alright, you got a deal." Rau'f stuck his hand out for Tata to shake.

She placed her small manicured hand in his and shook it firmly. Rau'f pressed a button on his desk and gave instructions to bring $275,000 to his office.

"Tata, I see something in you that I haven't seen in any woman that I have ever met," Rau'f stated, sitting on the desk right in front of Tata. She could see his dick print pressing against his slacks.

Tata didn't feel comfortable with him sitting in front of her like that, so she rose to her feet and walked around the desk to check out the Tank Anglaise for the last time before she depart from it. Rau'f watched her backside. Her black jeans hugged her firmly.

"How am I different from any other woman that you have met?" Tata said, picking up the watch.

"The glare in your eyes tells a story of a bloody betrayal that could only birth the heart of a savage. Most women fuck on their back to put food in their stomach, but not you. You too strong for that, too prideful. That savage in you motivated you to pick that tool up and go get it. I don't look at you as weak. I look at you as strong as they come."

Tata was taken aback by what Rau'f was conveying to her, but she was in boss mode and she refused to let Rau'f see her in any other light other than a boss. "So what, are you psychic?" Tata said nonchalantly.

"Never that. I just seen the telltale signs before."

"I thought you said I was a woman that you never met before," Tata said, placing the watch back down on the desk.

"Yeah, I seen the signs before, but just not in a female. The story your eyes tell often lies in the male being. But I want to give you a once in a lifetime opportunity," Rau'f said, getting up off the edge of the desk and facing Tata.

"And what's that?" said Tata, thinking that Rau'f wanted to make her his side piece or some shit that was going to degrade her as a woman.

Rau'f took a long pause before he spoke. "I need someone removed from position," Rau'f finally spoke, watching closely to see Tata's reaction to his statement. To his surprise, Tata didn't flinch.

"Why you can't handle your own business? I'm sure you got shooters on standby. Why not use them?" Tata switched her weight to one foot to the next.

"The hit can't come from me directly, so I need some outside assistance," Rau'f said.

Tata realized this could be a good for her and the Red Bottom Squad. But she needed to know more about the situation and what Rau'f was offering.

"What's in it for me?" Tata said, taking a seat behind the desk and letting her bottom find a home in his leather seat. She placed her Red Bottoms up on the desk and leaned back in the chair and waited for Rau'f's response.

Rau'f thought about how sexy Tata looked in his chair with her Red Bottoms up.

"Soon there will be some people that will come to D.C. and try to corner the drug market in D.C., but if somehow the guy that's running the trade is hit, then that would cause the outsiders to rethink their plan to take over the city and give me and my people time to get in position to lock this city down." Rau'f stuck his hands in the pocket of his Fendi slacks and continued to talk. "Now if you can handle this for me, the price is unlimited and I promise you a partnership in my organization."

Tata heart was beating fast. So much was running through her mind. She needed time to digest the info Rau'f was giving her. "I hear ya talking like a boss." Tata smirked, trying to keep her composure. "Who's the target?" Tata asked.

Rau'f took another long pause. He fished his iPhone out of his pocket. He tapped some keys on his phone. He handed the phone to Tata.

Tata took her feet off the desk and retrieved the phone from Rau'f. A handsome face was staring back at her. The male looked to be in his late 30's or early 40's, clean cut with a charming set of eyes. "And who am I looking at?" Tata asked.

"That's the infamous Cain," Rau'f retorted, placing his hand behind his back.

Tata's heart did a double pump in her chest. She swallowed hard. *Damn, this shit deeper than rap,* Tata thought to herself.

Rau'f studied Tata intently. A soft knock came at the door. Fidel, Rau'f's shooter, came in carrying a gray backpack.

"It's all there, boss," Fidel stated. "But we have a problem. The chick that came with Tata is requesting that Tata come out immediately."

Tata looked at Rau'f's security monitor and saw Phatmama holding court with two of Rau'f's people. Tata could tell by Phatmama's body language that she was getting ready to turn up. Tata jumped up and grabbed the bag from Fidel.

"Listen, Rau'f, I'm very interested in the propositions that you offered me. I will be in touch about the matter soon," Tata said, strutting out of Rau'f's office. Her Red Bottoms clicked against the tile. Tata wondered what the fuck was going on with Phatmama.

CHAPTER 21

Whip had been grinding double time with pushing the work he bought from Tata. He was on his third brick of heroin. The trap at Johnny Boys was doing numbers out the gate. The homies even opened a little dope spot on Nova Avenue. Shit was a little slow, but the spot had potential to good as the spot in the Big 3-0. Whip even put some dope down around Georgia and Park Road. He let Ink work the spot along with Clip, Mack-truck, and Bullet.

Whip hustled hard to take his mind off of Tata. Ever since their sexual encounter, Tata had been acting different. She was not taking his calls and when it was time to re-up, she sent Racks to drop the brick of heroin off and to pick the money up. He wasn't feeling how Tata was treating him, even though their relationship was strictly business.

Whip didn't even know why he was feeling the way he was feeling. The more he tried to block Tata out of his mind, the deeper her hooks sank into him. The business had proven to be good with the Red Bottom Squad, but he hadn't had to unleash his young shooters and that was a plus, because every nigga knew that you couldn't make money and go to war at the same time. It was either one or the other. So with that in mind, Whip stacked his paper. He had major plans for his Blood line. The money was coming in fast, but with all the mouths he had to feed, the money wasn't coming in fast enough. With three dope spots, the D.C.B.'s were making $15,000 daily. Whip wanted to double that, so he started putting out the word that he had grams and ounces of dope. Now the weight was not as potent as the dope he was selling due to him cutting it, but the product was good enough to keep the dope boys coming back and the fiends in a good nod.

Whip pulled up on the corner of Georgia and Park Road and got out of his Charger. Bullet ran up to the car and grabbed the McDonald's bag that held 500 bundles of dope and disappeared in a cut a few buildings down. Each bundle of dope held ten $10 bags of dope.

"What it do, Blood?" Boot said, walking up and dapping Whip up.

"Ain't shit, Blood, still trying to build this nation."

"Man, I'm feeling that, and we going to get there. The money is coming in," Boot said excitedly.

Whip made eye contact with Ink, who was standing across the street in front of the building. Ink threw up his B's on his hand and Whip returned the gesture. "What's up with that nigga Ink?" Whip asked.

"He think he's smarter than the average rabbit," Boot stated, gritting his teeth. Boot was in his body how Whip was letting Ink play up under him, but Whip was his big homie, so he let shit be for now.

"Good. Keep it that way, but watch the nigga," Whip said as he hopped back in his Charger and pulled away from the curb.

*****

"It's about time you bitches got here!" Zoey said as Tata and Phatmama climbed into her truck.

"Zoey, what the fuck is going on, and why are we here at my sister's complex?" Being in Tina's complex made Tata realize that she was a bad sister. She'd been so busy dealing with other shit she hadn't called her pregnant sister or even put together a baby shower for her.

"Okay, remember back at Rico's funeral?" Zoey said, sparking a Backwood.

Just hearing the words "Rico's funeral" made the hairs on Tata's and Phatmama's necks stand up.

"Yeah. What about it?" Phatmama asked.

"Well, remember Ski brought her male friend with her to the funeral?"

"That was the young nigga that I caught Ski fucking in my bed. Why? What about him?" Tata chimed in.

"Just listen. After the shootout at the cemetery, I seen a cocaine-white Lexus creep through the cemetery."

"Okay, and?" Tata said, kind of confused as to what Zoey was getting at.

"Look!" Zoey pointed at a white Lexus sitting on the other side of the apartment complex. "That's Ski's dude's Lexus and that's the same Lexus I seen at the cemetery. I just seen Ski and that same nigga at the funeral get out that Lexus and go in Tina's apartment. "

"You think that nigga had something to do with the shooting at the cemetery?"

"I'm damn near sure he had something to do with the shooting, but I'm wondering did Ski know anything about it?" Zoey threw her assumption out there.

"Well, if he had something to do with it, then why would the killa say, 'This is for Rocco'?" Phatmama said while studying the white Lexus.

Tata's brain was doing back flips in her skull from the conversation she had with Rau'f about Cain to now with the Lexus and cemetery shooting linking all back to Cain. She knew that this was not a coincidence. Cain was definitely tied to this shit.

"It's obvious, Phatmama, the nigga who drives the Lexus got some ties to Rocco and Cain. We just got to figure out how and use it to our advantage to get at Cain," Tata said, getting out of Zoey's truck to grab the bag of money that Rau'f just gave her. She took ten bands out of the bag and left the rest in her whip. "Listen, Phatmama, I'm gonna go find out what I can. Take my ride and go to my crib and put the money up. Me and Zoey gonna pay my sister a visit. We will hit you when we leave."

"Hell no, I'm going in with y'all!" Phatmama protested.

"Please, Phatmama, let me go in and see what the fuck I can find out," Tata said with authority in her voice.

Phatmama was hesitant, but she nodded her head in agreement. She climbed out of Zoey truck and got in Tata's whip and pulled out.

Zoey and Tata checked their weapons before they made their way to Tina's apartment. Zoey scanned the parking lot. It was fairly empty. Zoey could see the hustlers posted in the next complex over. Tata knocked on Tina's door and she could hear her niece Ski's voice coming through the door.

"Who is it?"

"It's me, Tata!" Tata said in her best loving auntie voice.

Tata and Zoey could hear some movement behind the door. The door didn't open immediately. It took a full two minutes before the door opened and Ski stood there nervously with her hand on her hip.

"Hey Auntie."

"Hey Auntie, my ass. What took you so long to open the door? You acted like you wasn't going to open it," Tata said with an attitude, walking past Ski with Zoey on her heels. "Where your pregnant-ass momma?" Tata asked.

As if on cue, Tina came wobbling her ass from the back room with a look of disgust on her face.

"Hola, mami," Tina greeted her nonchalantly. Tina was never the type to hide her feelings and it made it easy for Tata to read her.

"Oh My God! Look at you," Tata said, crossing the room and kissing her oldest sister on her cheek and touching her swollen stomach.

Tina cringed under Tata's kiss and touch. She tried to be discreet and remove Tata's hand from her stomach, but Tata caught the gesture.

"Damn, mami, I know that I haven't been the best sister, but you don't have to be like that with me. I'm here to try to make it right."

"Is that right?" Tina said, walking over to the love seat.

Zoey scanned the living room for any sight of Ski's little friend, but there was none. She peeked in the kitchen, but no sign of him. "I need to use the bathroom," Zoey said, making her way to the restroom that was located down the hall. Zoey had visited Tina's apartment a few times so she knew the set up.

"Yeah, that's right. I been making moves for us," Tata stated, pulling the ten bands out of her pocket and handing them to Tina. "I been putting shit together so we don't have to depend on a nigga to take care of us."

"Just like you don't need Rico no more?"

"What? Where the fuck that came from?" Tata snapped, getting in Tina's face.

Tina stared straight ahead. Her eyes looked through Tata. Tina eyes welled up with tears as she rubbed her stomach.

"Mami, where the fuck all this shade coming from?" Tata asked.

Tears spilled over the rim of Tina's eyelids and down her cheeks.

Quickly Tata's mind traveled back to the day of Rico's funeral and the way Tina acted at the funeral. Tina was carrying on like she had lost a lover versus a friend. She was laying over Rico's casket bawling her eyes out. Tina had turned back to Rico's casket, wiping her tears with the heels of her hand, and placed a kiss on the lid of his casket, leaving a deep red lipstick imprint of her lips behind.

Coming out her memory lane, Tata's eyes held her own set of tears. Tata had known Tina to participate in some shady-ass shit in her past, but what she was thinking that her sister may have done was the ultimate betrayal.

"Tina, whose fucking baby are you carrying? And don't give me that fuck shit about it's the nigga Cam's baby because I ran into that nigga last week and come to find out his ass was over in D.C. jail fighting a gun charge," Tata lied. She never ran into Cam. Her nose flared as she tried to get the truth out of Tina.

"What does it matter whose baby I'm carrying?" Tina mumbled and wiped her tears away from her face.

"Bitch, on every muthafuckin' thing I love, mami, if you don't tell me whose seed you carrying, I'm going to rearrange you teeth and stomp that fuckin' baby out cha."

"You ain't gonna do shit to my mama," Ski said from across the room where she watched the whole situation unfold.

"Stay in your lane, Ski," Tata informed her niece without even looking at her.

Zoey came down the hall from the bedroom. Tata was still looking at Tina.

"Speak on it, mami."

Tina's face turned into a ball of hate. "You murdered the father of my child!" Tina screamed in Tata's face.

It seemed like the air in the room became stale for about twenty seconds. Everything seem to freeze in the room. Zoey wasn't sure that her ears heard Tina right. The saying the hand is quicker than the eye seems to be true. Before anyone in the room could see it coming, Tata slapped spit out of Tina's mouth. They heard the slap before they saw it.

"You funky-ass bitch!" Tata struck Tina again across her face.

Tina struggled to get out of the love seat. Her large belly slowed her down. Ski couldn't stand by and let Tata handle her mother like that. She rushed Tata's back, catching Tata with a haymaker, stumbling Tata. Tata caught her balance on the arm rest of the love seat. She was seeing red that her niece swung on her while her back was turned. She pulled her Glock from the small of her back. Tata pointed the gun at Ski. Her niece's eyes got big as golf balls. Tata's chest rose and fell heavily.

"Tata, don't hurt my daughter!" Tina said, finally making her way to her feet.

Tata flipped the gun around and grabbed it by its barrel. She took two steps towards Ski and brought the handle of the gun across Ski's forehead.

"Agggggh!" Ski yelled out.

"Bitch, didn't I tell you to say the fuck in your lane, huh?" Tata said, bring the gun down on Ski's head again.

Ski crumpled to the floor. Tina screamed for Tata to stop.

"Please stop, Tata. Please stop!"

Zoey heard a door open up down the hall. She saw Ski's boyfriend come out of Ski's room with a burner in his hand. She upped her own gun.

"Nigga, drop it or I'll drop you," she said in her shooter stance.

"What the fuck going on in here?" Diego said, still holding his gun.

"Drop the fucking gun, nigga," Zoey warned Diego again. She had the ups on him.

Diego had his gun at his side. Diego wasn't with dropping his tool, but from where he stood, he could see the beat down that Tata was putting down on Ski. He didn't have a choice. He let the gun fall next to the Air Max's that he wore on his size 10 feet.

Tata tucked her Glock and went to putting hands on Ski. Tina couldn't stand by any longer. She rushed Tata's back, swinging wildly, catching Tata with a few blows to the side of her head before she yanked her by her Brazilian weave that she had in an eight inch ponytail.

"Get the fuck off my daughter!" Tina screamed and yanked Tata's ponytail with all her might.

Tata winced in pain. "Bitch!" she yelled as she fell backwards, leaving Tina to stand over her.

Tina attacked like a pit bull. She swung a hammer fist down on Tata then tried to jam her fingernails in her eyes. Tata moved her head from side to side, avoiding Tina's attack on her eyes. One of Tina's fingers slipped into Tata's mouth. Tata bit down on it, cutting through Tina's finger like steak and stopping once her teeth hit bone.

"Aggggggggh! Aggggggggh!" Tina cried out.

Zoey had trouble keeping her eyes on Diego and Tata at the same time. The only good thing about the situation was Ski was beat into submission. She laid balled up in a knot on the floor, holding her bleeding face while her mom and aunt duked it out. When Zoey turned her head briefly, Diego stepped his left foot over his gun. Now his tool rested between his feet.

Tata still had Tina's finger in her mouth. She could feel and taste her sister's blood in her mouth. Tina mustered up the strength and came down on Tata's face with a hammer fist.

The blow dazed Tata. Tina's badly bitten finger slipped from Tata's vicious bite. Tata went for her Glock, but the dizziness from being struck in the face so hard had her slow and disoriented. Tina knocked the gun away from Tata with a kick. Tina was in fight or flight mode. Tata had killed the only man she loved. She would be damned if she let Tata kill her and Ski or her unborn child. Tina rained blows down on Tata, making contact to her face and forearms. Tina dove for the gun that fell out of Tata's hand.

Zoey turned her head and saw Tina going for the gun. This distracted her enough for Diego to make his move. Diego kicked his gun into the room he came out of and dove in the room behind it. Zoey panicked and she let her Glock .40 ride. The gun thumped in her hand. The Glock bullets knocked chunks out of the drywall. Diego scooped his burner up and stuck his hand out the door without looking and finger fucked his trigger. Even though Diego couldn't see where he was shooting at, the bullets he busted from his gun whizzed past Zoey's head, making her take cover on the far right side of the living room.

The gunshots made Tina stop going for Tata's gun. She looked up from the floor next to her daughter. She looked spooked lying there shielding her stomach. Tata got her composure and grabbed her gun and stood up on wobbly legs. She looked at Zoey, who put one finger to her lips, telling Tata to be quiet. The only thing that could be heard was Ski crying. Zoey and Tata were trying to get their bearings and listen for Ski's boyfriend's next move.

They knew that they didn't have long. The way the gunshots erupted in the apartment, someone had to hear them and call the police. They heard light movement coming from Ski's room followed by the sound of a window rising. Tata made her way down the hallway towards Ski's room. Her heart banged in her chest. She went low in the room, gun out. The room was empty of human life. The bedroom window was open, but she made sure it wasn't a trick. Tata checked behind the door, under the bed, and in the closet, before she determined Ski's boyfriend was gone.

Tata came back in the living room, where Zoey was standing over Tina and Ski. Hate ran though her veins towards her sister. She didn't have time to deal with Tina, but she wasn't going to leave until she got some answers.

"Sit your ass up," Tata said, nudging Ski with her Red Bottoms.

Blood seeped from Ski's head wounds. Tata kind of felt bad for her niece. Ski was only doing what any daughter would've done, and that was protect her mother. Ski sat up and wiped blood from her eyes.

"Do you want to live?" Tata asked, pointing her gun at Ski. Ski nodded her head up and down.

"Please don't hurt my daughter, Tata," Tina cried from the floor beside Ski.

"Hoe, shut the fuck up!" Tata ordered. She turned her attention back to Ski. "I'm going to ask you a question, Ski, and you better tell me the truth. Do you hear me?"

Ski moved her head up and down.

"That nigga that was in here…that's your boyfriend, right?" Ski nodded her head up and down again for the third time. "Is that the same nigga that I caught you with at my house?"

"Yeah!" Ski barely said. Her voice came out in a whisper.

"What's his name? And what dealings he have with the nigga named Cain?" Tata asked.

Ski paused. She was hesitant for some reason.

"Bitch, spit it out, we don't have all day," Zoey chimed in. She was getting impatient. They had to get the fuck out of there.

Finally Ski spoke. "His name is Diego and Cain is his uncle. Please don't hurt my boyfriend," Ski pleaded.

Tata ignored her. She turned her attention to Tina. "You fucked my man and you carrying his seed. If you wasn't with child, I would murder your ass without mercy. But believe me, from this day forth, you are dead to me," Tata stated and walked out of Tina's apartment, leaving Tina to feel like shit.

Jibril Williams

CHAPTER 22

Jelli laid across her bed feeling like her girls had betrayed her. She felt that Tata pushed her out of the Squad too easily, almost as if she already had plans to get rid of her. To make matters worse, when she left, no one from the clique came behind her or called to check up on her. She couldn't understand why it was so easy for them to cut ties with her.

Tata really done lost her damn mind, Jelli thought to herself as tears ran down her face. Snot dribbled in and out of her nose as she cried. All she had now was Cain to love her and to bond with. She wasn't going to lose Cain for nothing in the world. Jelli was going to confess all her sins to Cain so if something ever came up in the future, it wouldn't take him by surprise. Jelli wiped her tears with the back of her hand. She sat up in her queen-sized bed and placed her feet on the floor. She leaned over and grabbed tissue out of the box and blew her nose. Next she took Cain's weed stash out of the night stand and rolled a fat Garcia Vega wrap. She lit her Kush incense and blazed the Vega.

Rain began to hit the window as a breeze rushed in the window. The breeze felt good against her skin. The purple lace boy shorts that Jelli had on were eaten up by her thick butt cheeks. Once the breeze pushed against her matching teddy, the texture of the silk fabric made her nipples bud. She took a long pull from the Vega and closed her eyes. Jelli let the smoke out through her nose and took another hit.

A set of arms folded around her waist, scaring the shit out of her. She almost choked on the weed.

"Relax, baby, it's me," Cain said with his baritone voice, placing his face in the crux of Jelli's neck.

Jelli hadn't heard Cain come in, but she was glad that he was home. She took another hit of the Vega and leaned her head back onto Cain's chest. Cain rubbed his hands over Jelli's smooth thighs. The softness of her skin aroused him. He placed kisses on the top of her head. Cain wrapped his arms back around Jelli's waist and squeezed her tight. Her Gucci perfume made Cain want to taste her. Jelli closed her eyes. She needed Cain's touch.

Tonight she needed his touch more than anything. She took

another hit of the Vega before she turned around in Cain's arms, facing him. She buried her face in his chest and wrapped her arms around him. Cain's hand found the best part of Jelli's body and he took a handful with both hands and massaged Jelli's mammoth butter soft ass. Just the feeling alone made Cain want to pick Jelli up and fuck her in the middle of the floor. He lifted Jelli's face from his chest to partake in a kiss. He was shocked to find Jelli's face covered in tears. Concern fell across his face.

"Baby, what's wrong?" Cain asked, still holding Jelli's face in his hands.

Jelli looked up at Cain with sad eyes. Her hand trembled as she put the Vega to her lips and inhaled a few times before she passed it to Cain. She grabbed Cain by the hand and led him to the foot of the bed, where she took a seat and motioned for Cain to sit beside her.

He could tell that Jelli had something heavy on her mind. He was thinking she was getting ready to announce she was pregnant or some shit. Even if she did, it wouldn't have mattered because was Cain was ready to start a family with Jelli.

Cain kicked his Versace slip ons off his feet and removed his diamond cufflinks from his shirt cuffs. He took a pull of the Vega. "Jelli, what's good? Talk to me," Cain said, placing a hand on her thigh. Smoke seeped out his mouth as he talked. "You know whatever it is, I got you. You not in it alone," Cain reassured Jelli.

Jelli faced Cain. She looked in his deep brown eyes and sighed. "After I tell you who I really am, you're not going to want to fuck with me, but I got to tell you who I am because I have fallen so in love with you."

Jelli's statement made Cain a little uneasy. He was wondering was he laying up with the cops or even worse, the fucking Feds. All those things raced through his mind, but he had to play it cool until he heard what Jelli had to say.

"Naw, baby, nothing would change how I feel about you," Cain stated, making eye contact with Jelli and giving her thigh a reassuring squeeze.

Jelli's eyes misted over as she gathered her courage to confess her sins to Cain. "I'm a member of the Red Bottom Squad," Jelli said, putting her head down.

Cain reached over and lifted Jelli's chin up with one finger. "What is the Red Bottom Squad, some type of girl club? You said that name like it's supposed to have meant something to me. Baby, whatever you got to tell me just say it, baby."

Jelli wiped a single tear from her eyes. Cain could tell that she was hesitant. "I rob jewelry stores and I just robbed a bank. That's what the Red Bottom Squad is all about. We rob shit and run that bag up."

Jelli told Cain everything from the beginning to end, including how they killed Rico.

*****

The cognac burned Tata's throat as she took a swig straight from the bottle. The Hennessy added heat that was already fermenting in her body from the bullshit with Tina. She wiped tears from her face. Tata hated that Tina betrayed her in such a manner and the fact that she killed her sister's unborn child's father didn't make matters any better.

Tata took another swig of Hennessy. She refused to let the situation take a toll over her. Tina chose her side when she opened her legs and let Rico in between them. There had been rumors in the past when they were young teens that Tina seduced one of their mother's boyfriends.

The word was that Tina got caught fucking her mother's boyfriend in her bed, but when Tata confronted her mother about the rumor, her mother didn't confirm or deny it. All she said was "Those without sin should cast the first stone." Tata now knew where Ski picked up the trait of fucking in other people's beds. They say the apple don't fall too far from the tree. Tata also remembered there was a time that another rumor had surfaced that Tina had fucked a group of niggas while visiting NC for bike week. Tata didn't know if this was true or not because she wasn't there. She was at home getting over the flu. But now every shady shit she had heard about her sister was true in her mind since she found out what type of hoe Tina really was.

"You alright over there, Tata?" Phatmama asked, blowing smoke out her nose.

Tata hearing her name being called brought her out of her daze. "Huh?"

"You good?" Phatmama asked again.

"Yeah, I'm good. I'm just fucked up about my sister getting pregnant by Rico and on top of that, us killing her unborn child's daddy."

"Shit, don't even let that shit take you on a guilt trip. This is the fucking life we live. Shit happens, and we had no idea that Rico was her child's father," Zoey said, chiming in.

"I understand that, but shit still got a bitch feeling a certain way. But I really want to know how the fuck Tina knows I killed Rico. Tina said it like it was without doubt she knew that I did it." Tata took another sip of cognac and wiped a hand over her face in frustration.

"There's only one way to handle this shit, Tata. If Tina is that fuckin' gone off Rico, no telling if her silly ass will go to twelve about what she thinks happened to Rico. Whether she has proof or not, we still don't need twelve looking into us. We be in too much shit for that," Phatmama spoke her mind about the situation.

Tata didn't want to entertain the thought of her having to kill Tina, and if she had to pop Tina, she would have to smash Ski's ass right along with her, because Ski just wasn't going to sit back silently and let someone kill her mother. Tata had to buy some time to figure out what was the best move.

"I got something that I need to discuss with you all. I really called this meeting to discuss the fact Rau'f offered me the opportunity to do a job for him that may change our lives forever. Rau'f offered me a spot in his organization."

The room held on to every word that came out of Tata's mouth. Zoey wondered what Rau'f could offer Tata that they didn't already have. Billie and Racks were confused as to who Rau'f was. But Phatmama knew the full potential of the situation that Rau'f was offering.

"It seems that we are not the only ones that want Cain dead," Tata spoke, taking another drink from the Hennessy.

"Shut the fuck up, Tata!" Zoey blurted out.

"Naw, I'm not lying. I found out that Cain is having some outside people coming in to take over his drug empire. Rau'f wants to take control of the D.C. drug trade. He's not in a position to do so at this time. But if we can hit Cain, it would give him enough time to get his people in position for the takeover. He is claiming that the hit gots to come from the outside of his organization, and that's where we come in at."

"Shiiid, let's do it. We trying to kill Cain anyway!" Zoey stated.

"But what kind of position Rau'f offering you?" Phatmama wanted to know.

"It doesn't matter what position he's offering. I'm not going to take it. All I'm going to ask is that Rau'f finance a few business ventures. I'm talking about lucrative strip clubs and an escort service. I want to take over the D.C. night life. You know that I can't work for no one. I got to be my own boss," Tata stated.

"So we taking the hit on Cain?" Zoey asked.

"Yeah, but I'm not mentioning to Rau' f that we already on Cain's line to kill him," Tata retorted.

"But where does this leave D.C.B.'s once Cain is dead?" Racks questioned Tata.

"Don't even trip. Whip will still be getting his issue on the heroin with a lower price," Tata conveyed.

Racks felt better with Tata's answer. She was feeling the Red Bottom Squad, but her loyalty was with her Blood family.

Tata's burner phone rang and she checked the caller I.D. It was Cee-Cee calling her. Tata rolled her eyes. "Racks, I need you to handle that Cee-Cee business for me."

"I'm on it. It's already in the making," Racks confirmed.

"When everything is said and done, tell Whip to come through and pay me a visit."

"I gotcha."

Tata picked her phone up and sent Cee-Cee a quick text. "Tomorrow" was all she texted. A few seconds later, a reply came through and it said "OK".

Tata took another sip of cognac. She was buzzing good. "Until we kill Cain, we are going to put our next lick on hold," Tata instructed.

Her thoughts went back to Tina. She was running the notion through her brain if she should kill her sister or not.

CHAPTER 23

Cee-Cee checked the time on her smartphone for the fifth time since she had been parked on the side of Roosevelt High School. She was paranoid as fuck for some reason. She kept having this feeling that someone was watching her, but she pushed the inkling to the side because she had gone through the FBI investigation with flying colors. The Feds had no clue that she was the inside man in the Bank of America heist. When the Feds came with their questions, Cee-Cee played the victim to the T. Being the bank's manager had granted her the privilege of getting inside details about the bank. This was a lick that she had put together for Rico and Tone, but with Rico now being deceased and Tone on the run for a minute, Ce'Anna, better known as Cee-Cee, asked Tata if she knew a few goons that were savage enough to rob a bank. Tata had assured her that she knew the right people who could pull the robbery off.

Cee-Cee gave Tata the inside scoop on the bank, everything from time and date to when would be the best time to hit the bank for the out of circuit money that the bank was holding. The only regret about the robbery that Cee-Cee had was how Tata didn't tell her that it was going to be her that would be robbing the bank. But what really pissed Cee-Cee off was how Tata and her people came in the bank and just straight up slaughtered Nick and his son. Cee-Cee thought that shit was uncalled for. Cee-Cee expressed how she felt about the ordeal and demanded a bigger cut of the heist money.

Cee-Cee wanted to break Nick's wife Karen off a little something for her loss. Tata wasn't having it at first, but then she broke down and agreed that was the best thing to do.

The time on her phone read 11:30 p.m. Cee-Cee was at home laid up under Tone getting piped down when she received a phone call from Tata's people telling her to meet her at Roosevelt High School to pick up her share of the money. At first Cee-Cee refused and told the caller to set something up for tomorrow morning. But the caller informed her that she and Tata were heading out of town on business and they would be gone for the next two weeks. So if she didn't retrieve her money now, she would have to wait until they get back from out of town. Cee-Cee wasn't about to wait another two weeks to get her money. She had places to go and shopping to do.

Cee-Cee caught hell trying to get out of her apartment. Tone was against her leaving her crib at eleven something at night to go meet with Tata's peoples. He wanted to ride along with her, but she refused his offer. She needed him at the apartment to watch over her daughter Nikky just in case she woke up. Tone finally agreed that he would watch Nikky until Cee-Cee got back, but Cee-Cee had to promise that she would suck his dick and lick his ass for the good deed of him watching her daughter while she ran out. Tone's freaky side made Cee-Cee wonder about him at times, but she agreed and hit the door.

Headlights entered the parking lot. Cee-Cee couldn't wait to get her hands on the money. A white Ford pickup pulled next to her Kia. The window on the passenger side of the pickup rolled down.

"You Cee-Cee?" a dyke chick with tats on her face asked.

"Yeah, that's me!" Cee-Cee said through her cracked window.

Racks got out of the truck with a black & green Gucci bag. Cee-Cee popped the locks on her doors. Her guts bubbled with nervousness. The driver of the truck got out and climbed in the back seat of Cee-Cee's Kia. He settled in behind her. Racks got in on the passenger side.

"What's good, Cee-Cee?" Racks asked.

"Hmm, nothing, just trying to get this money so I can get back home to my daughter and my man," Cee-Cee said, checking the guy sitting behind her out through her rearview mirror. The two strangers placed an unnerving feeling in her car. She wanted to pick her money up and be gone. She didn't understand why Tata's people even got in her car.

Racks dropped the Gucci bag on Cee-Cee's lap. Cee-Cee greedily opened the bag to inspect the money. The little light that the school parking lot provided illuminated the money that was overflowing out of the bag. The money looked funny in the light.

"It's all there," Rack stated, checking her side mirror.

"I hope so. I'd hate to have to call Tata and cuss her ass out about my money. I'm still pissed for how she cut up in the bank," Cee-Cee retorted.

144

"Yeah, I heard about that. Tata wanted to holla at you about that. She wants you to call her once you got the money in your possession," Racks informed Cee-Cee.

"I'll call her once I get home and get this money counted."

"Naw, baby girl, you need to call her now," Racks instructed in a serious tone.

Cee-Cee rolled her eyes and grabbed her phone to call Tata. Tata picked up on the first ring.

"Hola, mami," Tata's voice boomed through the car from Cee-Cee having the phone on speaker.

"Tata, what's going on? Your people are demanding that I call you," Cee-Cee said with much attitude.

"I just wanted to thank you for your service."

"Tata, you could've thanked me another time. I got shit to do," Cee-Cee stated firmly.

"See, that's the fucking problem. A bitch be trying to show love and unite on some women in power shit and you stupid-ass bitches got to disrespect a boss by complaining about how she does shit. But one thing I'm not going to accept is you talking about tipping off the police if I don't give you a bigger cut."

"Tata, I'm not trying to hear that shit!" Cee-Cee said, cutting Tata off.

"Okay, you don't have to hear me, but just let me say this one last thing. That money you got is not your cut. That's what I call blood money," Tata said.

Cee-Cee looked down at the money and back at her phone that she held in her hand. "Bitch!"

It was Cee-Cee's turn for her statement to be interrupted. A rope was slipped over her head from the dude that sat behind her. He pulled back hard on the rope. The rope cut into Cee-Cee's skin. Ink planted his feet firmly on the floor and stood with his back pressed hard against the back seat. He pulled it and held it there. Cee-Cee fought to get air in her lungs. She tried her damnedest to get her fingers in between the rope and her neck, but Ink had the rope pulled too tight.

"Ock! Ock!" Cee-Cee choked. The veins in her eyes popped from lack of oxygen.

Ink took a deep breath and pulled harder on the rope.

Cee-Cee began kicking wildly. Tata could hear Cee-Cee fighting for her life on the other end of the phone. She smoked a Vega with her eyes closed and imagined that what was transpiring on the other end of the phone was happening to her sister Tina.

Cee-Cee thrashed and jerked. She worked her foot up and stood on the horn with her foot. The loud blare of the Kia horn made Racks grab Cee-Cee's feet from the steering wheel and hold them while Ink continued to strangle Cee-Cee. Ink gritted his teeth and pulled back harder on the rope. Finally Cee-Cee's body went limp.

Racks reclaimed the Gucci bag and Cee-Cee's smartphone that had fallen on the floor. Ink was still strangling Cee-Cee when a figure appeared next to the car. The masked man holding a Mack 10 scared the shit out of him. The masked man wore a red bandanna over the lower part of his face. Ink wanted to go for his strap that was on his waistline, but he still had his hands entwined with the rope that was around Cee-Cee's neck. Even if he could have gotten to his gun, it would have taken an act of Congress to have gotten a shot off due to the Mack 10 that was pointed right in his face.

Whip pulled the bandanna down from the lower part of his face and Ink's ass broke wind. He already knew what the lick read. He had tried to kill Whip some weeks ago. He saw Whip trailing Spoon one night. He knew that Whip was on his line to dome check Spoon about him getting Racks' cousin killed and for running off and leaving Racks when the police ran down on her. Ink made a mistake and thought that Whip didn't see him that night when he was on Spoon's line. It was obvious that Whip did, because he was now standing over him with his hammer. Ink tried to kill Whip because he embarrassed the shit out of him in front of the homies by making a dope fiend that he got caught tricking with bite him on the dick.

Racks jumped out of the car without saying a word. Boot came up on the passenger side of the Kia brandishing a Mack 10 of his own.

If Whip and Boot thought that Ink was going to beg for his life like a bitch, they had him fucked up.

"What the fuck y'all gonna do? You going to squeeze them triggers, or you going to suck my dick?"

146

Whip's and Boot's Mack's got to jack hammering in their hands. The weapons riddled Ink's body. His corpse jumped and jerked in Cee-Cee's back seat. They emptied their clips into Ink, spilling his DNA all over Cee-Cee's car.

"A hard lesson!" Whip whispered as he hopped in the waiting pickup truck with Racks and Boot.

*****

"What the fuck! Aw man, no-no-no-no!" Tone watched from the street where his car was parked. He watched two men run down on Cee-Cee's car and drop helluva rounds in her whip. It seemed like they were never going to stop shooting.

When Cee-Cee told him that she was going to meet Tata's people to pick up some money, he waited until she left the apartment and snuck out with a sleeping Nikky and followed Cee-Cee. He was hoping that he could follow Tata's people and they would lead him straight to her.

But shit went haywire. He just witnessed the only woman that he loved get gunned down.

"Naw, fuck that!"

Jibril Williams

CHAPTER 24

Racks maneuvered the pickup truck through traffic. She pulled around 7th and Taylor, where she ditched the stolen truck for her Delta 88.

"You seen that nigga trying to go out like a G, Blood? I wish I could have had some time with him. I swear I would've had the nigga begging for his fuckin' life," Boot stated.

"I know, right? But sometimes you just got to handle the business and keep it mobbing," Whip retorted. When Racks told him about the business she had to take care of for Tata, she expressed how she wanted to hit Ink at the same time, so they came up with a plan to have Ink kill Cee-Cee and they killed Ink. Some classic hood shit.

"Tata said the bag belongs to you and Boot. She wants you to come past her crib when we are done," Racks said as she pulled behind her Delta 88. She was promising herself that she was going to upgrade in the car department soon.

Whip took the bag and handed it to Boot, who jumped into Racks' car with her.

"I'm about to slide through there now," Whip stated as he walked to his Charger that was parked in front of Racks' car.

Racks and Boots threw up their Blood signs and murked out.

Whip got in his car and twisted up a fat Vega. He adjusted the sounds in the Charger and Wale & Jeremih's track "On Chill" came through his speakers. He was feeling the beat and the melody. Whip eased the Charger into gear and headed to Tata's apartment. He wondered what Tata wanted. He didn't know what to expect. This would be his first time seeing her since they had fucked. She still wasn't returning his calls. Just to see what the lick read, he texted Tata two simple words: "En route," and to his surprise, he immediately got a reply: "I'll be waiting." Whip didn't know what to make of the situation dealing with Tata, but he was definitely going to find out tonight.

*****

Tone gritted his teeth as tears fell down his face. Snot dripped from his nose. He tried to keep the white pickup in sight without its occupants seeing him. He wiped his face dry with his shirt. He peeped in the back seat at a sleeping Nikky and the sight of her only made him madder.

Suddenly the truck made a left turn on Taylor Street and Tone got caught at the red light. "FUCK!" Tone said in frustration as he banged his fist on the steering wheel. He knew by the time the light turned green, Cee-Cee's killers would be long gone. He wasn't going to give up.

Two full minutes had passed and finally the light turned green and Tone made the left onto Taylor Street. He didn't speed up the next block up. He scanned the street for the white pickup that he had seen not too far from the corner of the block.

A red Charger sat in front of the pickup. Once Tone made it to the Charger, he observed someone sitting in the car twisting a blunt with a red bandanna around his neck. Tone knew then he had his man. Tone pushed his car to the middle of the block and double parked beside a brown F150. He grabbed the 44 that was tucked under his right thigh. He glanced back at a still sleeping Nikky. She was still resting peacefully on the back seat of Tone's car. She was sleeping like an angel who didn't have a clue when she woke up she would be waking up to a nightmare.

Tone exited his car and started making his way back towards the red Charger. A car entered the block and the Charger pulled away from the curb.

"Fuck!" Tone said angrily as he watched the Charger drive right past him. He wanted to open fire on the Charger, but a car was closely driving behind the Charger. Tone couldn't afford any witnesses, so he dashed back to his car to follow the Charger for a better shot.

*****

Whip whipped his Charger into a parking spot in Oak Crest Towers. He shot Tata a quick text letting her know that he had just pulled up. She replied back stating that she was on her way out. A dark-colored Kia had just pulled into the parking lot and parked at the far end of the parking lot. Whip saw the car and was waiting for its occupants to exit the car, but they never did.

Tata exited her building wearing a pair of snug-fitting light blue jeans and pair of black Red Bottoms with a black Fendi shirt. Seeing Tata stirred something up in Whip. He was in awe and frustrated all at the same time. Tata motioned for Whip to get out of his car and into her truck. Whip followed suit. It was a little awkward-feeling inside Tata's truck once they met each other there.

Whip didn't greet Tata. Tata was the one that wanted to meet, so she was entitled to lead the conversation well as the greetings.

Tata reached in her purse and removed about fourteen grams of sour diesel and a pack of Backwoods wraps. She handed the items to Whip. Whip began the process of rolling the diesel up for their meeting.

"Thanks for coming, Whip," Tata said, breaking the silence.

Whip didn't acknowledge Tata's statement. He just continued to twist the Backwood up. Tata took Whip's gesture as somewhat offensive, but she keep talking.

"The last time we were together, some shit happened that shouldn't have taken place," Tata said, powering on her BOSE system and allow Rick Ross's "Summer Reign" to be heard throughout the truck.

"And why is that?" Whip asked, speaking for the first time.

"Because for several reasons. I don't want my team to view me as weak."

"Come on, Tata, keep shit 100. You don't want your people to see you fucking the help," Whip said, agitated, cutting Tata off.

The way that Whip made his statement sounded so harsh. Tata didn't want to offend Whip, but she had to stick to her guns.

"Absolutely!" Tata confirmed.

Tata outright admitting it made Whip feel a certain way.

"Tata, you got shit fucked up. Never would I be the help. Let's not get my assistance to you mistaken. I'm just here to help you as you help me. One hand washes the other. Regardless if you going to fuck with me or not on any level, I'm going to climb to the fucking top. It's in me to do so. That shit that happened was just a fuck. It wasn't like a nigga was trying to wife you or nothing," Whip said aggressively.

Tata let out a sigh. "Listen, we both can sit here and pop that tough shit at one another. I'm not going to lie. There's an attraction between us. The head was good and you got that king-ding-a-ling, papi," Tata said, laughing. Tata didn't want this tension between her and Whip. She just need Whip to understand her on her level.

Whip had to join her and partake in the laughter. "So what's really the problem?" Whip inquired. "All this can't be about you and your team or the fact that I'm a shooter for the Red Bottom Squad," Whip said, blazing the Backwood.

"I'm gonna to be honest with you, Whip, it's all of those things, and plus I can't allow myself to be conquered by a man again - not right now anyway. I just got out a controlling relationship. It had gotten so bad with the controlling shit I had to body my ex."

Shit became clear to Whip. Tata had been hurt. If he was controlling, then he was abusive to her as well. The two go hand in hand. But he also knew that Tata revealing killing her ex was done for a reason, and that was to let him know she wasn't going to let anyone hurt her again.

"I understand your struggle, Tata. I comprehend what you are going through. I don't think your team will lose faith in you to lead them by fucking with me. As long you keep them eating, they will follow you to the end of the world and back. You got a group of thorough-ass bitches on your team. For some reason, women's bonds are stronger than men's and that's because men always want to conquer shit that they know they shouldn't even process," Whip said, hitting the Backwood and passing it to Tata.

"So are we good?" Tata asked.

"Yeah, we straight, but let me ask you something. Can we just get to know each other better as friends? So we can have a better understanding of who we both are?" Whip said.

Tata thought about it for a minute. "I think that we can do that."

"And if you don't want to, we don't have to display our friendship to our people."

"As for now, I would like that." Tata inhaled on the Backwood. "Now since that's taken care of, I have some important matters that I need to discuss with you."

"Okay, shoot."

"Do you have any problems about killing a female or a child?" Tata asked. She studied Whip's face.

Whip was taken aback by her question. He was wondering if this was some type of trick question.

"D.C.B's don't pick and choose who gets it. If the order comes down, then it's executed," Whip spoke seriously.

Tata liked what she heard. She spent the next twenty minutes giving Whip the rundown on Tina, Ski, and her boyfriend Diego. Whip swore that the name Diego rang a bell in his head, but he couldn't place a face to the name. Tata wanted him to handle Tina personally. She didn't want anyone to know about the hit. Whip agreed and also let Tata know that he would have his shooters get on top of Ski and Diego. Tata informed him that she would text him Tina's address tomorrow and he could start there.

Whip caught movement on the parking lot. A nigga got out of the blue Kia. Whip's alarm bells started going off. That was the same car that had pulled in the parking lot behind him. *Damn, he just now getting out his car*, Whip thought. The dude was moving on the back side of the cars. Whip could see him clutching a chrome gun in his hand.

"Tata, you strapped?" Whip asked with seriousness.

"Yeah, why?" Tata replied with panic in her voice.

"Let me see that shit now!" Whip said, turning around, looking through the back window of Tata's truck.

Tata quickly fumbled with her purse. She handed Whip the burner. The Glock had a thirty round extended hanging out the bottom of it. Tata turned around in her chair, trying to see the threat Whip was seeing. She caught a glimpse of someone with a hat pulled low over his head walking on the backside of the cars that was parked on the back side of the parking lot.

Whip grabbed the gun from Tata and checked to see if it had one in the head. He cut the overhead light in the truck off so when he opened the truck door the light wouldn't alert the robber that Whip was getting out of the truck.

"Tata, start this bitch up!"

Tata hurried and started her truck up. Whip opened the door and planted his foot on the pavement. The shooter was about three cars away from her and moving stealthily with his head low.

Whip emerged fully from the truck. He was facing Tata with the Glock at his side. But his eyes were on the nigga creeping on the other side of the parking lot.

A police cruiser turned up into the Oak Crest Tower parking lot and stopped behind Tata's truck. Whip eased the gun under the passenger seat of Tata's truck.

"Tata, turn the truck off and get out, and make sure that you lock your doors," Whip quickly instructed.

Tata turned the truck off, stepped out of her truck, and hit the power locks button stationed on the truck's door panels and closed the door. Whip closed his door and walked around the truck and entwined his hands with Tata's hand.

The officer got out of his truck and made his way towards Tata.

"Hey there!" he greeted as her walked up on Whip and Tata.

Whip was hoping the officer wasn't the top cop type.

"Hey," Tata returned the officer's greeting.

"What you two got going on tonight? I got a call saying that someone was just sitting in front of the building in a strange car. Do you all live here?" the officer asked with his hand rested on the handle of his gun.

Tata could tell that the officer was ready to shoot if he had to. She and Whip had peeped how the gunman on the other side of the parking lot had ducked down behind the cars when the police pulled up.

"Wow, someone called the police on us?" Tata said. "Me and my boyfriend just came home from a late movie. We was just sitting in the truck having a light conversation, but anyway, I do live in the building," Tata confirmed.

The officer looked from Tata to Whip. He looked at the bifocals that Whip had on his face and drew the conclusion that the couple wasn't up to anything. Officer Walker was familiar with the Oak Crest Towers. He knew after certain hours of the day you needed a key card to get in the building. And if the couple didn't have a key card that meant that they didn't live there.

"Do you have a key card to get in the building?" Officer Walker asked.

"Yes, I do," Tata stated, holding up the white key card that was attached to her key chain.

You could hear a car engine turn over in the parking lot. Whip saw the blue Kia pull out and drive past them and the officer. The driver never looked their way.

"Okay, you both have a nice night," the officer said, walking back to his car.

Tata and Whip watched as the Kia's taillights turned out of Oak Crest Towers.

CHAPTER 25

"Shit!" Tone whispered. He wanted to smash the nigga that killed Cee-Cee so fucking badly. Talk about bad timing. Who would have expected for the police to have shown up at that particular time? He took that as a sign that the time wasn't right to avenge Cee-Cee's death.

Tone needed to figure out what he was going to do with Nikky. He wasn't in a position to be taking care of a child, but he owed it to Cee-Cee to make sure that Nikky was taken care of. But at the moment, he needed somewhere to go until he figured shit out. Going back to Cee-Cee's crib was a risk he couldn't take.

Now that he had gotten a line on Tata's funky ass, he soon would be able to get his money and start putting some money moves together. He couldn't believe how Cee-Cee's assassin led him straight to Tata. "So that's where you laying your head at, huh? Oak Crest Towers," Tone spoke to himself.

He knew where he could go until he figured shit out. He didn't know how Tina was going to react when he showed up at her door with a sleeping Nikky in his company, but fuck, he need her to G the fuck up and respect his gangsta.

*****

Jelli had been looking down at her phone for the last twenty minutes, trying to decide if she was going to call Tata and ask her to come to her man's party. Cain had been pressing her to invite her friends to his get together. He told Jelli that his party was going to be a memorable event for them so she had to invite her close friends. Jelli informed Cain of hers and Tata's falling out, but he insisted that the event would iron out any misunderstandings that they may have had. So Jelli promised Cain that she would invite the Red Bottom Squad. She just hoped that she and Tata could get along throughout the event. She had already reached out to the rest of the girls. They all promised to be at Bass & Cru tomorrow to turn up. All Jelli had to do now was call Tata.

Jelli hit her contact info for Tata's number. Tata's phone rung about six times before she answered it.

"Hello?"

Jelli was trying to feel energy to see if Tata was bothered by her calling or not because Tata never answered her phone without checking to see who was calling first. "Hey Tata!" Jelli said nervously. "Are you busy?" Jelli asked.

"Naw, just here talking to Whip. Why, what's up?"

"Well, I was wondering if you are still going to come to Bass & Cru tomorrow. Remember my man is throwing an event there. He wanted to meet my friends," Jelli said, bracing herself for the conflict she knew Tata was going to bring.

"I already heard from Phatmama about the event. I'm going to come through and show my support. I owe you a sit down anyway. We got to have a meeting of the minds, so I will see you tomorrow. And be ready to turn up like old times."

Tata's statement had a hint of excitement in it. Jelli closed her eyes and thanked God for Tata's acceptance.

"Thank you, Tata. See you tomorrow night. He rented the whole club out. So call me when you get to the club so I could meet you at the door with your passes."

"Okay, I will," Tata said, disconnecting the call.

*****

"What happened to you?" Tone said as he walked into Tina's apartment, seeing all the black and purple bruises that decorated Tina's face.

Tina ignored Tone's question and embraced him, holding on to him for dear life. Tone hugged Tina back while he carried Nikky in his arms.

"How is my baby?" Tone asked.

"He's fine," Tina replied. Her lips found Tone's and she kissed him softly.

Tone reach down and took a handful of her ass.

"I miss you, Tone. I have been worried about you like crazy. I have so much shit to tell you, papi," Tina said, leading Tone to her bedroom.

CHAPTER 26

Jelli stepped out of Cain's Bentley Bentayga looking sexier than a muthafucka. The champagne-colored custom made Chanel dress was like new skin on her. It hugged her curves as if she was born in the dress. The dress showed off much cleavage and a lot of leg.

You couldn't tell Jelli that she wasn't the Bossman's top bitch. She wore her hair in a straight ponytail that was braided all the way down her back. The end of her ponytail rested comfortably on her big ole booty. Her black Chanel purse matched nicely with her black Red Bottoms. Jelli had spent most of the day being pampered and prepped for this event.

Cain had spared no cost for Jelli. He made sure she had spa time, got her nails, toes, and hair done, pussy hairs trimmed. And to top everything, off he had a professional makeup artist come and do Jelli's makeup.

"Oh nawl, bitch. Who the fuck are you fucking and do he have a brother or something? This nigga got you riding a muthafuckin' Bentley!" Phatmama said, standing next to her truck with Zoey, Billie, Racks, and Tata.

Jelli embraced her girls one at a time. Tata sat back and watched her team love on Jelli before she stepped in and hugged Jelli. She kissed Jelli on each cheek.

"Damn, mami, I see that you are looking good. You wearing that Chanel piece."

"Thanks!" Jelli said to Tata, turning around in a full circle so Tata could check out the whole dress. "It's custom made too."

"Hold the fuck up! The dress is custom made by Chanel and you riding a Bentley. Oh yeah, I definitely gots to meet this nigga," Zoey said.

The whole group broke out in laughter. Jelli handed everyone a club pass. The passes had V.I.P. on them.

Phatmama was lighting the night up with her all-red Gucci romper. Her Brazilian weave was braided in two thick cornrows that trickled down her back. The all-black Gucci handbag matched great with her own pair of black Red Bottoms that occupied her size 8 feet.

Billie came to show the fuck out, strutting hard in her all-black leather Christian Dior body suit. Billie was getting all type of cat calls while making her way to the club's entrance. The way that her southern curvy body filled out the outfit was like someone with an extra-large hand had squeezed into an extra small glove. Every curve and crease could be seen. Even the impression of Billie nipples and clit pressed against the leather outfit. Her yellow Red Bottoms highlighted her one piece outfit right along with the matching Christian Dior purse that she carried. Women were envying Billie because of the purse. It was hard as hell to find the purse in that color and they knew if they could have found the purse, it would have cost them a grip to get it. The men were dying to know who the white chick was with the black woman's body. Tata had to smile and smirk at some of the crazy-ass comments that niggas were throwing Billie's way.

One guy even yelled out, "Hey Vanilla, would you like some chocolate chips in your vanilla ice cream?"

Billie took it all in stride.

It seemed like every dope boy, every hustler and crime boss had come out to support Jelli's man. The parking lot was full of foreign cars. Porsches, Aston Martins, BMW's, Lexuses, and 600 Benz's decorated the parking lot. Someone even came to the event in a drop top Phantom.

Tata's club attire was simple. She wore a pair of white Prada pants with a matching blouse. She chose to focus on her accessories. Her right wrist was draped in a rose gold Rolex with a black diamond bezel. This piece was a deceased Rico's. Tata had a few links removed from the watch band so the Rolex could fit her wrist perfectly. She wore a pair of rose gold earrings. Tata had a light coat of MAC lip gloss on her lips. She was ready to turn up tonight. Even though she just got with her girls, she felt good being with them.

"Damn! Zoey, if you don't pull that dress down a little farther, you going to make a nigga act a fool tonight," Racks said, teasing Zoey.

Zoey's Versace dress with the Medusa head on it was short and form-fitting. You could see the brown bottom part of Zoey's volleyball-size butt cheeks. She had to keep pulling her dress down after every few steps. Her sex appeal was all the way up tonight and it didn't make matters better with her sucking and twirling a grape-flavored Blow Pop in her mouth as she walked.

"Racks, don't start no shit. If you start tripping tonight, you won't never taste this pussy again. And you already know I like dick more than I like pussy," Zoey threw that out there.

"What the fuck!" Jelli yelled out.

"Girl, you ain't know Zoey been let Racks tap that?" Phatmama said, laughing.

"Umm, excuse me. This is not the time and place to discuss who I'm giving my pussy to," Zoey commented, rolling her eyes.

Racks could care less what the women were thinking about them. She couldn't take her eyes off Zoey's ass.

Jelli and Tata looked at each other and shook their heads. Tata shrugged her shoulders.

"Here go your passes," Jelli said, handing the women the V.I.P. passes. "These passes allow you to drink and smoke for free, request certain songs to the DJ, and to use the private bathroom without waiting in line. Also the passes allow you to leave and get back in the club without getting pat searched."

The women passed by the bouncers with ease after showing them their passes.

The club was packed. It seemed like everyone had some type of bottle in their hands as they two stepped or rocked with the music that the DJ had pumping out of the club speakers. The men in the club were draped in top of the line clothing labels. The women in the club were half-naked, trying to secure a boss for the night or even better, for a lifetime. A club waitress had on a skimpy see-through one piece that showed off her nipples and coochie. She was pushing a small cart that held 24 gold bottles on it. Jelli stopped the waitress.

"Give me and my friends a bottle apiece!" Jelli yelled over the music.

The waitress frowned. "I'm sorry, but these bottles are for the group over there!" The waitress pointed to a group of dudes in a corner that were turned all the way up. They had about six strippers in front of them who were clapping and slinging booty everywhere while the group poured champagne and twenty dollar bills over their wet naked bodies.

"If you can pop and twerk your ass like them strippers, you can join them," the waitress stated sarcastically.

"No thank you, boo-boo! But get them another round of bottles. These right here are for my fam," Jelli said, grabbing bottle after bottle off the cart and handing them to Tata and Phatmama.

The waitress grabbed Jelli's hand, stopping her from passing any more bottles out. Jelli's hand froze.

"Bitch, unhand me."

"Like I said, these bottles are for them gentlemen over there," the waitress stated firmly.

Jelli yanked her hand free from the waitress's grip. Jelli removed a white card that was sticking out from between her breasts. Her club pass was different from the ones that she had given her team. Her pass was white and it had BOSS BITCH plastered across the front of it. The waitress's eyes got bugged.

"I'm sorry, I'm so sorry!" the woman stuttered. She immediately started handling out more bottles to the Red Bottom Squad.

Jelli looked at her with a smirk on her face and with disgust in her eyes. The woman hurriedly made her exit.

"Damn, what you got going on in here?" Zoey said. "You pulling out V.I.P. cards and bitch starts bending to your will."

"My boo gave me this card to keep the help in check and remind them that I'm the King's Queen," Jelli said, popping a bottle of Ace of Spades. She turned the bottle up to her lips. The squad did the same. "Red Bottom Squad in the building!" Jelli yelled out, holding her bottle in the air.

"Red Bottom Squad!" the group repeated.

The women made their way to a section of the club that was designated for them. The area was roped off. The women ordered more champagne and a few Hennessy shots. Jelli ordered some blueberry Kush to be brought to them and some Vega wraps. The girls got lit. The DJ dropped a Dreezy joint featuring T-pain, "Close to You", and the girls went off.

"Oh shit, that's that joint! Let's dance, y'all!" Phatmama screamed out.

The women hit the dance floor, bottles in one hand and a burning Vega in the other. The women sang along with Dreezy with their arms in the air. They seductively moved their hips to the rhythm of the music. It seemed like all eyes were on them in the club. The niggas in the club had for some reason formed a circle around them and took in the assets.

"You niggas can look, but you better not touch!" a voice came booming through the speakers.

Tata and the group started looking around, trying to figure out where and who the voice was coming from. Jelli stood there with all her teeth showing because she knew that it was none other than Cain letting niggas know she was spoken for.

Cain came walking out in the crowd with his nephew Diego and his right hand man Fate. Cain was wearing a black tailored Giorgio Armani suit. The silk shirt that he wore under the suit jacket was the same champagne color as Jelli's dress. The Ferragamo boots he wore had him looking like he just stepped out of *GQ* photo shoot. Tata's heart drummed in her chest at a rapid pace. Phatmama's hand went to her waist, but she realized her gun was in her purse. Zoey clenched and unclenched her fist.

"Hey baby! Jelli said, hugging Cain. "These are my girls right here."

"I finally get to me the infamous Red Bottom Squad," Cain said, extending his hand to the women.

They all seemed to hesitate, but they all accepted his warm handshake. Tata was taken aback by how Cain knew them as the Red Bottom Squad. That was a testament that Jelli had been pillow talking with this nigga.

"Nice to finally meet you also. You are more handsome in person then what Jelli has described to me," Tata said, trying to play shit cool.

Cain smiled at Tata's compliment. "Oh, this is my nephew Diego and this my brother from another mother right here. This is Fate," Cain introduced his people.

Phatmama and Diego were having a stare down with one another. It was like no one was in the room but them. Diego nodded his head at the group and turned on his heels. Cain frowned at his nephew's rudeness. Fate stayed posted beside his boss.

"I hope that you all have been enjoying yourselves," Cain stated.

"Yeah, we are having a ball. But can I ask you, what's the occasion?" Zoey asked with her nosy ass.

Cain smiled and grabbed the bottle and Vega from Jelli's hands and passed them to Billie. He escorted Jelli to the stage.

"Excuse me! Excuse me. Ladies and gentlemen, may I have your attention? I have an announcement to make," Cain said into the microphone.

The music faded out and the club occupants started to gather around the stage.

"As you know, I'm king of this city!" Cain said and the club roared and cheered. Once the crowd calmed down, Cain continued. "A king isn't really a king until he has crowned a woman as his Queen!"

Jelli's hands shot to her face. She couldn't believe what was happening.

"Fuck no!" both Tata and Phatmama mumbled. None of the other girls had put it together that Jelli's man Cain was the Cain they were contracted to kill and the same Cain that had been trying to kill them.

Cain unbuttoned his Armani suit. Cain took a knee on the stage floor and pulled a blue ring box out of his pocket from Tiffany's. Jelli's hands trembled as she held them to her face. Cain opened the ring box and the most flawless ring stared back at Jelli. A four karat diamond sat on a platinum band. The diamond was bigger than any diamond that she or the Red Bottom Squad had ever heisted. "Jellica Robertson, would you do the honors and be my wife?" Cain asked.

Jelli was overwhelmed. Tears of joy started cascading down her cheeks, destroying her professional makeup job, but she didn't give a fuck. She knew Cain loved her, but never enough to consider as a wife.

Tata, Phatmama, and Zoey looked on with stone faces. So much shit was running through Tata's mind. She wondered did Jelli know Cain wanted Phatmama dead, and if that was why she been acting distant with the team and wanting to cut her ties with the Red Bottom Squad. If Jelli agreed to marry Cain, then the shit was what it was.

Jelli wiped the wetness from her cheeks and grabbed the microphone from Cain. She cleared her throat. "Bae, I would love to be your wife."

The club roared in cheer and a few women in the club slammed their glasses to the floor and stormed out of the club cussing. Tata immediately got her phone out of her pocket and sent Rau'f a quick text.

"Is the offer still open for the Cain job?" Tata texted.

"I concur!" was what Rau'f replied.

Tata then sent Whip a text explaining the situation.

Cain placed the ring on Jelli's finger and tongued her down nice and hard. They shared a kiss that seemed to last forever. Finally Cain released Jelli and announced drinks were on him for everybody. Once again the club roared in cheer. The DJ played an old joint by Jagged Edge, "Let's Get Married", which was on point for the current situation.

Cain whispered in Jelli's ear, "Baby, go show your friends your ring and enjoy your night. I got some business to handle in the back. I will catch up with you in a few minutes."

Jelli was dying to get back to her girls and show off the ring. She was going to be the first out the group to be married. She remembered when they were on lock in federal prison they used to fantasize about who would get married first and what their wedding days would be like.

Jelli kissed Cain intensely once again before she broke away from his lips and rushed towards her girls with her hand in air with her diamond leading the way for all to see.

"Oh my God! I'm getting married!" Jelli said, dancing in front of her friends while waving her hand in front of their faces.

But her friends weren't basking in the same joy she was and she picked up on it quick. "What's the matter? I know you bitches ain't hating on me?"

Tata and the group took Jelli to the private bathroom so they could talk in private.

Jelli couldn't understand what was going on. She knew that one of these bitches wasn't getting ready to tell her that they were fucking with Cain on the inside or some crazy shit like that, but she knew that something was right.

The Red Bottom Squad got Jelli in the bathroom. Tata wasted no time breaking down the situation to Jelli. She told Jelli about how Phatmama had robbed Cain's cousin Rocco and how Cain had sent his goons at the cemetery to kill them. Tata failed to mention that she accepted a contract to kill Cain.

Jelli could remember a few months ago Cain's cousin getting killed and robbed, but she never knew that it was Phatmama behind it. Jelli knew her friends were having this talk with her for a reason and that was her to pick and choose sides.

Anger overtook Jelli. "Every time I find happiness, you bitches always find a way to destroy it. I'm not letting you destroy this for me. I love Cain. You all just going to have to leave until I can talk with Cain."

CHAPTER 27

Cain stood at the back of the club. He watched his queen being escorted to one of the private bathroom by her friends. They must wanted to go and get the low down on him in private. He took a sip of Hennessy Black from the shot glass. He was taking a moment to himself before he met with the group elite hustlers of D.C. He was going to break the news of his retirement to them and ensure them they were going to be in good hands. They were going to be mad, but they would get over it. Cain thoughts turned back to Jelli and her friends. He must admit Jelli's friends were some bad muthafuckas. He still couldn't believe that these bitches were robbing banks and jewelry stores.

"Yo, Unc, we need to talk," Diego stated, interrupting Cain's thoughts.

"Can it wait? Because the way you're looking I know it's going to be some bullshit," Cain said.

Diego handed Cain a photo, a photo that Cain was way too familiar with. He had given the photo to Diego months ago. It was a picture of the woman that had killed and robbed his cousin Rocco. Seeing the picture brought nothing but pain to him and swiftly he wanted to murder something. A hint of anger jumped into Cain's eyes when he look at Diego.

"You bring me this bullshit on a night like tonight? You still gunning to fill Rocco's position. I told you before you have it once you find the bitch that killed Rocco!"

"I brought you this shit tonight because I have found the bitch who killed our fam, and I brought it to you because I see that you getting ready to marry the fucking opts. Jelli is friends with the chick in the picture. The bitch in the picture is the redbone wearing the red romper. Her name if Phatmama," Diego said.

Cain looked at the picture and back towards the private bathroom, where Jelli and her friends were coming out. Cain overlooked the fact that Jelli seemed distress. He was focused on Phatmama and sure enough, the woman in the picture was her.

A blaze of fire was set in Cain's eyes. He understood Jelli words more clearly now. *"After I tell you who I really am you're not going to want to fuck with me."* The words been haunting Cain for days now. That night when Jelli confessed about the Red Bottom Squad, he felt like it was more than that she wanted to say, but chickened out at the last minute. She must have wanted to confess about Phatmama killing his cousin.

Cain jumped on the phone and told Fate to round up the security team.

*****

"Jelli, hold up, let me talk with you!" Tata said, trying to grab ahold of Jelli's arm.

She yanked away from Tata and kept mobbing through the crowd of people. The girls could see Cain and Diego at the back of the club. Their body language was screaming that they were onto them. Tata's phone vibrated on her hip. She saw that it was Whip telling her that he and Boot were outside.

"Let's get out this bitch!" Tata said, pushing her way through the crowd. She glanced to her right and her sister Tina was staring at her from the bar, but what had her confused was why she was hugged up under the nigga Tone. She didn't have time to investigate the matter. She wanted to get ghost before Jelli had a chance to make it back to Cain and tell him what she knew.

The group made it out to the parking lot. She was relieved to see that Whip and Boot were out there waiting on them. "Y'all good?" Whip asked, holding a Mack 10 in his hand.

"Yeah!" the women answered.

Cain and his team came running from the back of the club. They were about nine deep and they were strapped too.

Boot saw them coming. "It's a hit!" Boot yelled out, which sent the girls to drawing their guns.

"Suu Wuu!" Whip gave the call and about fifteen Bloods popped up off the side of parked cars with red bandannas tied around their faces.

Cain's men got it popping.

BOOM-BOOM-BOOM-BOOM
BLOCKA BLOCKA BLOCKA BLOCKA

The D.C.B.'s weren't ducking no rec either. It was a work call. They returned fire.

Two of Cain's men were cut down. The AR-15 round found a home in the shooter's chest, flipping him. The other gunman was hit with a head shot. Phatmama was banging her Glock, standing right next to Boot. His fo'-fifth racked off. The two traded shots back and forth with Cain's men. The Bass & Cru parking lot was a battlefield. There were so many shots being fired you couldn't count them all.

Tata had fallen onto the pavement. Whip shot at everything that didn't have a red bandanna around his face. He saw one of his little homies take a shot to the face and that shit just made him madder. He squeezed rapidly on the Mack 10 trigger. YAK-YAK-YAK-YAK.

Tata made it to her feet and she kept her head low and made it to her truck. There was a brown package taped to her windshield. Billie and Racks made it back to their car. The guns were smoking and empty.

Cain was volleying shots back and forth with Phatmama and Boot. All he had on his mind was killing Phatmama. Boot's fo'-fifth slug slammed into his shoulder and stomach.

Zoey was running toward Tata's truck when all of sudden the back of her head exploded, sending her body forward. She tumbled across the concrete of the parking lot.

"Nooooooo! Noooooo!" Tata cried out. She started banging her gun as she ran towards Zoey.

BOOM-BOOM-BOOM-BOOM...CLICK! Tata's gun was empty. She fell to her knees. "No, Zoey, please wake up, girl. You going to be alright!" Tata said as her hand trembled, rolling Zoey on her back.

Zoey had a gaping hole in her head. Rolling Zoey on her back didn't do any justice for her because all types of brain matter and blood oozed out the head wound. Zoey's skirt was up over her waist. She still held her pink Glock in her hand. Tata cradled her head and rock back and forth. "No, baby girl, not you, mami, not you!" Tata cried.

Whip knelt down beside Tata. "Come on, Tata, you got to leave her. We got to get out of here!" Whip said, pulling Tata by the arm.

She snatched away from him. The police sirens could be heard in the distance.

"Come on, Tata. We got to go or we going to fucking jail," Whip said, looking around to see if there were any more opts in the parking lot. The parking lot was decorated with bodies.

Tata took Zoey's pink Glock from her hands and straightened Zoey's skirt out. She pulled the skirt down over Zoey's lace panties. She didn't want them to find her friend with her goodies all out in the streets. She kissed Zoey's forehead and closed Zoey's eyelids. "I swear, mami, they going to pay for this," Tata whispered.

Tata and Whip jumped in her truck after Whip snatched the package off the windshield. They bailed out of the parking lot before the police got there.

*****

Cain played dead on the on pavement until Jelli ran over to him.

"Oh baby, please be alright."

Cain opened his eyes as Jelli touched his face. He hated the bitch, but he knew that his only chance of finding Phatmama was through Jelli, so he had to play his role.

"Get me some help, baby! I'm bleeding out," Cain stated. His insides were on fire due to the bullet that had penetrated his stomach.

Police cars pulled up to the club from all angles right along with a squad of paramedics. Jelli flagged the paramedics down.

"Over here. You have one over here. He is still alive," Jelli instructed.

The medics jump out and assisted Cain. "Sir, what's your name?" the medic asked.

"Cain Ross."

They loaded him into the ambulance. Jelli tried to hop in with Cain.

"I'm sorry, ma'am, but you can't ride with us."

Jelli didn't want to argue with the paramedics. She wanted to get Cain to the hospital soon as possible. "Okay, I will follow you all there," Jelli said, climbing off the back of the ride. Jelli ran and jumped in Cain's Bentayga and followed the ambulance. Jelli was praying for Cain as she followed the ambulance.

They had gotten about six blocks from the club when a dark blue truck cut the ambulance off. Somehow, a car had ended up getting between Jelli and the ambulance. A masked woman jumped out of the truck, pointing a bronze-colored Mack 10 at the ambulance. The rig couldn't back up because of the cars that were behind the ride. The masked woman rushed to the back of the rig.

"Open this bitch up!" She shot a few rounds in the door of the rig.

The paramedic hurried and fumbled with the door latch. The ambulance door swung out and the two medics spilled out of the rig and took off in flight. The shooter climbed in the rig and stood over Cain.

Cain stared up in fear. Only seconds had passed, but it felt like forever to Cain. Cain believed a man should have a right to look his killer in the eyes before they killed him.

"Show your fucking face!" he yelled out. But he was hoping that someone would save his ass.

The masked woman pulled her Jason hockey mask up and Cain stared into the eyes of Phatmama. She leveled the Mack face level to Cain and whispered, "Red Bottom Squad, bitch!"

YAK-YAK-YAK-YAK-YAK!

Jelli watched from her car two cars back.

THE NEXT MORNING

Tata opened the package that Whip and taken off her car. She was still a nervous wreck from last night. Everyone from her team had checked in except Phatmama. All she could do was hope that Phatmama was alright. The death of Zoey had the team shook up and wanting blood.

A burner phone was in the package. It had a note attached to it and it read VOICEMAIL. Tata turn the phone on and there was a voice mail there waiting for her. She hit play and what she heard made her heart thump like a bass drum.

It was a male voice. "I want five hundred thousand or I will give this recording to the police. I know you killed Rico."

Then she heard her own voice. "Rico, how does it feel to be at someone else's mercy?" Then you heard the fall of an axe chopping into Rico's body.

The phone fell from Tata's hand.

To Be Continued...
The Heart of a Savage 3
Coming Soon

Submission Guideline

Submit the first three chapters of your completed manuscript to ldpsubmissions@gmail.com, subject line: Your book's title. The manuscript must be in a .doc file and sent as an attachment. Document should be in Times New Roman, double spaced and in size 12 font. Also, provide your synopsis and full contact information. If sending multiple submissions, they must each be in a separate email.

Have a story but no way to send it electronically? You can still submit to LDP/Ca$h Presents. Send in the first three chapters, written or typed, of your completed manuscript to:

LDP: Submissions Dept
Po Box 870494
Mesquite, Tx 75187

DO NOT send original manuscript. Must be a duplicate.

Provide your synopsis and a cover letter containing your full contact information.

Thanks for considering LDP and Ca$h Presents.

Jibril Williams

Coming Soon from Lock Down Publications/Ca$h Presents

BOW DOWN TO MY GANGSTA
By **Ca$h**
TORN BETWEEN TWO
By **Coffee**
THE STREETS STAINED MY SOUL **II**
By **Marcellus Allen**
BLOOD OF A BOSS **VI**
SHADOWS OF THE GAME II
By **Askari**
LOYAL TO THE GAME **IV**
By **T.J. & Jelissa**
A DOPEBOY'S PRAYER **II**
By **Eddie "Wolf" Lee**
IF LOVING YOU IS WRONG… **III**
By **Jelissa**
TRUE SAVAGE **VII**
MIDNIGHT CARTEL III
DOPE BOY MAGIC III
By **Chris Green**
BLAST FOR ME **III**
A SAVAGE DOPEBOY III
CUTTHROAT MAFIA II
By **Ghost**
A HUSTLER'S DECEIT III
KILL ZONE **II**
BAE BELONGS TO ME III
By **Aryanna**
THE COST OF LOYALTY **III**

The Heart of a Savage 2

By **Kweli**

CHAINED TO THE STREETS II

By **J-Blunt**

KING OF NEW YORK V

COKE KINGS IV

BORN HEARTLESS IV

By **T.J. Edwards**

GORILLAZ IN THE BAY V

TEARS OF A GANGSTA II

De'Kari

THE STREETS ARE CALLING II

Duquie Wilson

KINGPIN KILLAZ IV

STREET KINGS III

PAID IN BLOOD III

CARTEL KILLAZ IV

Hood Rich

SINS OF A HUSTLA II

ASAD

TRIGGADALE III

Elijah R. Freeman

KINGZ OF THE GAME V

Playa Ray

SLAUGHTER GANG IV

RUTHLESS HEART III

By Willie Slaughter

THE HEART OF A SAVAGE III

By Jibril Williams

FUK SHYT II

By Blakk Diamond

Jibril Williams

THE DOPEMAN'S BODYGAURD II

By Tranay Adams

TRAP GOD II

By Troublesome

YAYO III

A SHOOTER'S AMBITION II

By S. Allen

GHOST MOB

Stilloan Robinson

KINGPIN DREAMS II

By Paper Boi Rari

CREAM

By Yolanda Moore

SON OF A DOPE FIEND II

By Renta

FOREVER GANGSTA II

By Adrian Dulan

LOYALTY AIN'T PROMISED II

By Keith Williams

THE PRICE YOU PAY FOR LOVE II

By Destiny Skai

THE LIFE OF A HOOD STAR

By Rashia Wilson

TOE TAGZ III

By Ah'Million

CONFESSIONS OF A GANGSTA II

By Nicholas Lock

PAID IN KARMA II

By **Meesha**

I'M NOTHING WITHOUT HIS LOVE II

The Heart of a Savage 2

By **Monet Dragun**

CAUGHT UP IN THE LIFE II

By **Robert Baptiste**

NEW TO THE GAME II

By **Malik D. Rice**

Life of a Savage II

By **Romell Tukes**

Quiet Money II

By **Trai'Quan**

Available Now

RESTRAINING ORDER **I & II**

By **CA$H & Coffee**

LOVE KNOWS NO BOUNDARIES **I II & III**

By **Coffee**

RAISED AS A GOON I, II, III & IV

BRED BY THE SLUMS I, II, III

BLAST FOR ME I & II

ROTTEN TO THE CORE I II III

A BRONX TALE I, II, III

DUFFEL BAG CARTEL I II III IV

HEARTLESS GOON I II III IV

A SAVAGE DOPEBOY I II

HEARTLESS GOON I II III

DRUG LORDS I II III

CUTTHROAT MAFIA

By **Ghost**

LAY IT DOWN **I & II**

179

Jibril Williams

LAST OF A DYING BREED

BLOOD STAINS OF A SHOTTA I & II III

By **Jamaica**

LOYAL TO THE GAME I II III

LIFE OF SIN I, II III

By **TJ & Jelissa**

BLOODY COMMAS I & II

SKI MASK CARTEL I II & III

KING OF NEW YORK I II,III IV

RISE TO POWER I II III

COKE KINGS I II III

BORN HEARTLESS I II III

By **T.J. Edwards**

IF LOVING HIM IS WRONG…I & II

LOVE ME EVEN WHEN IT HURTS I II III

By **Jelissa**

WHEN THE STREETS CLAP BACK I & II III

THE HEART OF A SAVAGE I II

By **Jibril Williams**

A DISTINGUISHED THUG STOLE MY HEART I II & III

LOVE SHOULDN'T HURT I II III IV

RENEGADE BOYS I II III IV

PAID IN KARMA

By **Meesha**

A GANGSTER'S CODE I &, II III

A GANGSTER'S SYN I II III

THE SAVAGE LIFE I II III

CHAINED TO THE STREETS

By **J-Blunt**

PUSH IT TO THE LIMIT

The Heart of a Savage 2

By **Bre' Hayes**

BLOOD OF A BOSS **I, II, III, IV, V**

SHADOWS OF THE GAME

By **Askari**

THE STREETS BLEED MURDER **I, II & III**

THE HEART OF A GANGSTA I II& III

By **Jerry Jackson**

CUM FOR ME I II III IV V

An **LDP Erotica Collaboration**

BRIDE OF A HUSTLA **I II & II**

THE FETTI GIRLS **I, II& III**

CORRUPTED BY A GANGSTA I, II III, IV

BLINDED BY HIS LOVE

THE PRICE YOU PAY FOR LOVE

By **Destiny Skai**

WHEN A GOOD GIRL GOES BAD

By **Adrienne**

THE COST OF LOYALTY I II

By Kweli

A GANGSTER'S REVENGE **I II III & IV**

THE BOSS MAN'S DAUGHTERS I II III IV V

A SAVAGE LOVE **I & II**

BAE BELONGS TO ME I II

A HUSTLER'S DECEIT I, II, III

WHAT BAD BITCHES DO I, II, III

SOUL OF A MONSTER I II III

KILL ZONE

By **Aryanna**

A KINGPIN'S AMBITON

A KINGPIN'S AMBITION **II**

I MURDER FOR THE DOUGH

By **Ambitious**

TRUE SAVAGE I II III IV V VI

DOPE BOY MAGIC I, II

MIDNIGHT CARTEL I II

By **Chris Green**

A DOPEBOY'S PRAYER

By **Eddie "Wolf" Lee**

THE KING CARTEL **I, II & III**

By **Frank Gresham**

THESE NIGGAS AIN'T LOYAL **I, II & III**

By **Nikki Tee**

GANGSTA SHYT **I II &III**

By **CATO**

THE ULTIMATE BETRAYAL

By **Phoenix**

BOSS'N UP **I , II & III**

By **Royal Nicole**

I LOVE YOU TO DEATH

By Destiny J

I RIDE FOR MY HITTA

I STILL RIDE FOR MY HITTA

By **Misty Holt**

LOVE & CHASIN' PAPER

By **Qay Crockett**

TO DIE IN VAIN

SINS OF A HUSTLA

By **ASAD**

BROOKLYN HUSTLAZ

By **Boogsy Morina**

The Heart of a Savage 2

BROOKLYN ON LOCK I & II

By **Sonovia**

GANGSTA CITY

By **Teddy Duke**

A DRUG KING AND HIS DIAMOND I & II III

A DOPEMAN'S RICHES

HER MAN, MINE'S TOO I, II

CASH MONEY HO'S

By Nicole Goosby

TRAPHOUSE KING **I II & III**

KINGPIN KILLAZ I II III

STREET KINGS I II

PAID IN BLOOD **I II**

CARTEL KILLAZ I II III

By **Hood Rich**

LIPSTICK KILLAH **I, II, III**

CRIME OF PASSION I II & III

By **Mimi**

STEADY MOBBN' **I, II, III**

THE STREETS STAINED MY SOUL

By **Marcellus Allen**

WHO SHOT YA **I, II, III**

SON OF A DOPE FIEND

Renta

GORILLAZ IN THE BAY **I II III IV**

TEARS OF A GANGSTA

DE'KARI

TRIGGADALE I II

Elijah R. Freeman

GOD BLESS THE TRAPPERS I, II, III

Jibril Williams

The Heart of a Savage 2

By Ah'Million

KINGPIN DREAMS

By Paper Boi Rari

CONFESSIONS OF A GANGSTA

By Nicholas Lock

I'M NOTHING WITHOUT HIS LOVE

By Monet Dragun

CAUGHT UP IN THE LIFE

By Robert Baptiste

NEW TO THE GAME

By **Malik D. Rice**

Life of a Savage

By **Romell Tukes**

LOYALTY AIN'T PROMISED

By Keith Williams

Quiet Money

By **Trai'Quan**

BOOKS BY LDP'S CEO, CA$H

TRUST IN NO MAN

TRUST IN NO MAN 2

TRUST IN NO MAN 3

BONDED BY BLOOD

SHORTY GOT A THUG

THUGS CRY

THUGS CRY 2

THUGS CRY 3

TRUST NO BITCH

TRUST NO BITCH 2

TRUST NO BITCH 3

TIL MY CASKET DROPS

RESTRAINING ORDER

RESTRAINING ORDER 2

IN LOVE WITH A CONVICT

Coming Soon

BONDED BY BLOOD 2

BOW DOWN TO MY GANGSTA

The Heart of a Savage 2